WHAT READERS ARE SAYING

"Wonderfully written, easy to read, captivating!"

"'The Train' is a must read! A definite page-turner! Andrea Hines makes a great correlation between a train ride and life, and its many stops and detours."

"I absolutely loved this story! I felt like I was part of the sister circle of friends. I couldn't put the book down. I had to find out what was going to happen! Great for a book club."

"'The Train' is an adventure. It made me laugh, cry and reflect on the benefits of having true friends. The author seemed to have the reader in mind regarding the years these women had known each other. It is a great book."

OTHER BOOKS BY AUTHOR

When He Whispers

Nanny Nuggets

When Life Speaks

THE TRAIN

Andrea L. Hines

Studio Griffin
A Publishing Company
www.studiogriffin.net

For information, contact:
Studio Griffin
A Publishing Company
Garner, North Carolina
studiogriffin@outlook.com
www.studiogriffin.net

Cover Design by Ruth E. Griffin
Images by © Black queen design/Adobe and Anton Barashenkov/Adobe

First Edition

ISBN-13: 978-1-954818-27-9

Library of Congress Control Number: 2022930796

1 2 3 4 5 6 7 8 9 10

Dedicated to those willing
to embrace life's journey with truth,
transparency and joy found in self-discovery

TABLE OF CONTENTS

CHAPTER 1
In The Beginning…
The Story Before The Story

We always speak of life as being a journey, and that it is. So, if you think about a journey, you think about travel. If you think about travel, there is a point where you begin, a point where you end, and many stops along the way. You think about planning where you're going, who you are traveling with, how long you will be gone, what you will take, and what you will leave behind. And of course, one of the most important questions: how will you travel? Will it be by car, plane, or train?

Traveling by train used to be my favorite. The sounds, the scenery, the sights—all part of 'going somewhere.' I've discovered that our life's journey is like the trains we ride and the roads we travel, especially when it comes to relationships, particularly romance and marriage. Okay, so you've probably guessed by now that I'm not going to tell a story about an actual train per se, but the many things trains, relationships, and life's pursuits have in common.

After seeing many of my friends marry and divorce, I found myself developing some definite views on marriage and weddings. After talking to many of my female and male friends, it seems there is always a period during the dating process that causes either party (or both) to reconsider the monumental life decisions they are making as it relates to long-term commitment, covenant relationship and marriage. When people meet and express an interest in pursuing the possibility of something more than a casual dinner date every now and then, there are a myriad of things to be discovered, discussed, and considered. But the truth isn't always factored into the process. In talking with one of my long-time friends right before the nuptials of a couple who had been dating for a while, we discussed relationships we knew had gone right and the ones that had gone terribly wrong. The ones that didn't have that 'better or worse' scenario that withstood the test of time seemed to have the same thing in common: key issues were not confronted with honesty. And once engaged, the relationship began to take on a life of its own. She described it like, "A train that never slows down. It just keeps picking up speed until it seems too risky, too much to lose, too dangerous to try and get off, even if you wanted to." What do you do when you know you need to stop the train before it gets to the station?

All of this was going through my head as I traveled back home—by train, of course—to connect with my three friends, Jean, Charlotte, and Diamond. It was a short ride, and the next day we would be catching another train to attend the wedding of our mutual friend, Samantha. Back-to-back train rides seemed a bit excessive, but for me it was going to be a joy to relax, maybe even an adventure. Anything could happen when the four of us got together.

At any rate, it was an absolutely perfect October afternoon. Leaves were just beginning to turn, and the autumn rainbow of foliage was spectacular. Gold, orange, bright red to deep burgundy, and all shades of green in between seemed to create a colorful canvas that decorated miles and miles of landscape along the railway. The weather was still warm for that time of year as the leaves gently floated to the ground. It was a second summer with temperatures that coincided with the picturesque scenery. So far so good. Then I remembered I was going to a wedding which, over time, had become one of my least favorite things to do in the entire world. Before you let out a deep heavy sigh, or gasp in utter disbelief as you attempt to determine what contributed to my major maladjustment of not liking weddings, let me explain a few things in my defense.

Don't get me wrong. I am not against marriage. I was married once, and I am always ecstatic when I hear a good love story. In fact, most of my friends are married—not necessarily happy but married. The others bailed on their marriages early on before they could inflict too much emotional damage on one another. A few have managed to work things out, hang in there, and hold on for dear life. They grimly describe marriage as hard work similar to that of an early 1900s chain gang. Yet they smile and say they wouldn't have it any other way. Go figure. Be that as it may, and even though I'm divorced, I still think marriage is the best thing going between a man and a woman who are spiritually grounded, have their priorities right, and can love like 1 Corinthians 13 says we should love. It might seem naïve, but I've seen it work and therefore I believe it can.

But I digress because that's another story for another day. Remember I said I'm not against marriage. That's not the issue. I'm not too fond of the wedding itself with all its pomp and circumstance, financial strain, and drama that rivals the old Bridezilla television program. I don't like the period leading up to and right at the wedding. Too many times, I've watched two beautiful people pledge the rest of their lives to each other with an awestruck look that vacillates between, "This is going to be the most amazing day of my life," and "What in God's name am I doing?" Those are the couples who concern me, the ones that didn't pay attention to the signs, the red flags that clearly indicated, "WARNING," but they've come too far to turn back, right? What would people think if they didn't go through with it, right?

So, they go down the aisle, ready to stand at the altar, and barrel right ahead anyway. They don't know what else to do. They can't help themselves. They can't stop now. Almost as soon as they say, "I do," they realize they don't. And they later part ways, broken and bitter. They enter into new relationships with old baggage and a cycle of, "Somebody's going to pay." It's like watching a potential train wreck and not being able to do a thing about it. The friend I mentioned earlier had another observation I found extremely interesting. She boldly stated, "On the way to the altar, you can expect to experience one of two things: more of the beautiful train ride or a disastrous train wreck. But when the engagement ring goes on your finger, that's your ticket for the train."

I want to pause here for a moment because I feel compelled to tell you a little more about why this journey called life reminds me of a train ride. You can board the life train at any point usually, depending on where you want to go. I think all of us are looking for a place where there is joy and fulfillment. I'm not talking about the fictional passages you write on the pages of your life as you settle for one thing or another to pretend you've arrived, but really experiencing it—true fulfillment and pure joy. You start at the station and travel the train marked for 'your' THERE. It's the destination that gives you everything you think you ever wanted. You believe when you reach your THERE, you receive the ultimate in everything you ever dreamed of. THERE is where it all happens. THERE is where you find everything you need or want on your happiness meter. For example, if you have always struggled financially and if you desire wealth, you board the *Prosperity Train* and you believe if you get THERE, your life will be amazing. You will have no financial worries when you get THERE. It's a place where money is never in short supply, where price tags are never an issue, and, "How much?" is a phrase totally missing from your vocabulary. If you can just get THERE.

For some, THERE is about being with someone. It's the *Commitment Train*, usually crowded because its passengers require so many stops along the way. True commitment passengers are not looking for an express. They want the stops along the way for self–assessment; learning to love; understanding forgiveness; and if they're smart, they'll take the lay-over at 'truth and transparency.' The final destination is marriage. That's where they say, "If I was married, I'd never be lonely again. I wouldn't have to bear the burdens of life alone. Someone would take care of me if I could just get 'there,' and my life would be forever changed for the better."

And of course, there's the *Romance Train* which is slightly different. It usually ends up at the same destination as the *Commitment Train*, but the stops are unique. These passengers are on more of an express journey that's not necessarily governed by wisdom, self-evaluation, learning about how to really love, etc. The stations on this route often include connections for Jilted Junction, Ex-Partners Expressway, or the layover at Chaos Crossroads and Betrayal Boulevard.

Then there are those 'Constantly In Pursuit Of…' and they usually board the *Success Train*. Their final destination takes a little time to decipher. However, once it's clear, they are all in because THERE will get them things (like the position, the title, the notoriety, influence, etc.) that are a part of what they think embodies what success is all about. If they can just get THERE, life will never be the same. Destination reached; dreams realized.

The only problem with THERE is it is never that simple and you miss an awful lot of wonderful things looking in one direction, while dismissing all the other things that make us who we are: all the encounters that shape our lives; the situations and circumstances that help us discover the things that are truly worthwhile; and the people who teach us and help us to grow. They are the ones traveling with us through life to get us THERE…or so we think.

CHAPTER 2
Once Upon A Time

The train arrived just before sunset, and I was glad to be home. I picked up a snack from the cafe at the station and grabbed a cab to my place of rest, a little worn, but not too weary. I was way too excited to do anything but think of the next few days ahead. What a weekend this was going to be! I decided to unpack and repack after I had eaten something. I had pretty much laid everything out before I left town, so it wouldn't take long for me to pull everything together. As I sat down to eat what was turning into the best sandwich on the planet after not eating all day, I realized how much I was looking forward to having lunch tomorrow with Jean, Diamond and Charlotte.

It seemed a little crazy to me that the four of us were more than mere acquaintances. We were all so different. I remember Jean saying one time that the only thing all of us had in common was their friendship with me. I hate to admit it, but I felt some kind of way when she first said it, but over the years it became more and more obvious that she was right. These were my grown friends, I guess you could say. I had three friends growing up who mirrored them, but we lost touch over time. We went our separate ways.

I sometimes think that maybe I was destined only to have three friends at a time. Perhaps that's all the drama I can handle, even as a kid. I remember in my junior high school years, my three friends and I seemed to have the same daydreams about what we thought romance was. We didn't know it, but we were already planning to one day ride that train: Girl meets boy who quickly becomes the boyfriend, best friend steals boyfriend, best friend betrays boyfriend, boyfriend realizes she was never meant for him, boyfriend returns to original girlfriend with pathetic apology (which she accepts, by the way), and somehow all is right with the world. No matter what we read or where the story was set, it was pretty much the same, with a variation here and there. At any rate, my first look at the not-so-happily-ever-after side of life came about on one Saturday afternoon with my friends at the time. Jackie (not short for anything, just Jackie), Dot (she was named after her Granny Dorothea), and pushy, loud-mouthed Teresa (who loved to introduce herself as "Teresa, no H.") None of us really cared for Teresa that much but she was a little older and had brothers—older brothers, *cute*, older brothers with friends, so we thought eventually the association would pay off, and on occasion it did. Even as girls, we had our own daydreams about getting married and reaching the happily-ever-after that the romance novels alluded to; and Saturday was our day to, "Ooh," and "Ahh," over something we'd read. We had our own book club and didn't even know it. We started talking about a book by Amy Porter, a writer of teen romance novels back in the day. All of her books had four major characters and each of us envisioned ourselves as one of them. It didn't really matter who we were, because each one of them always got the 'Man of Her Dreams'.

On this particular Saturday, things weren't quite the same. Dot and I were having a difference of opinion about the relationship between two of the characters in the book we were reading, and Hurricane Teresa stormed into our perfect setting.

"I can't believe it," she shouted. "This is one of the worst days of my life." Then out of nowhere, she let out a scream, and began to bawl. Not just cry or sob, but bawl, which I think is at the top of the list when it comes to your eyes leaking. We were shocked! No one had ever seen her even whimper, and I personally didn't think she had tear ducts. Here was our Teresa having an emotional breakdown before our very eyes.

"Good grief, Teresa," Dot shrieked, scared half to death. "What is the matter with you? Why are you screaming? What did I miss?"

"Whatever it is, I know we can't fix it," Jackie stated in her matter-of-fact Jackie way. She was like somebody's grandmother, always rational, always calm. You could almost hear a choir singing softly as she continued, "Besides, nothing can be that bad, and nothing is bigger than God."

Uh-oh, we all knew prayer was next. Even at a young age we knew we could count on Jackie and Jesus. As Jackie got ready to speak again, I'm sure I saw smoke rising from the top of Teresa's head as she balled up her fists, clenched her teeth, and said in a way that made us tremble, "You have no idea." I didn't know what she was about to say next, but I knew it was going to be better than anything we were reading in Amy Porter's books.

As Teresa paced back and forth, she began telling a story about the wedding of the century, or at least her version of it.

"You all know how long my sister, Brenda, has been planning her wedding, right?" She filled in the blanks before we could dare respond that we hadn't. "Of course, you don't. Well, anyway, it's been over a year, and I was going to be one of the junior bridesmaids, and my dress was gorgeous." The waterworks had turned on again. "Well, everything was just perfect, and I got home today only to discover I won't get to wear the dress at all."

"So, all this is because you can't wear the dress?" Jackie addressed her haltingly but genuinely concerned. "Do you have to get another one?"

Dot felt it was her turn to chime in with something uplifting to keep Teresa from convulsing. "I bet the next one will be even prettier. I mean, you look good in anything."

Teresa turned and glared at Dot furiously, saying, "Dot, I promise you if you say one more thing…"

Dot quickly lowered her voice, not at all sure what she did wrong, and softly said, "Look, I know you're upset, but you can get another dress—"

"IT'S NOT ABOUT THE STUPID DRESS," Teresa screamed at her.

It was my turn to speak up. Besides, I was probably the only person who could reach the decibels Teresa had managed.

"OKAY, IF IT'S NOT THE DRESS, WHAT IS IT?" I yelled. Everything got quiet. Well, whaddya know,

I thought. I had managed to bring some calm into this curious conversation. "Teresa, please calm down," I continued. I couldn't stop now. "You've got all of us scared. We've never seen you like this. Tell us what you need, but please stop crying. Like Dot said, you can find something else, I'm sure."

"There's not going to be a wedding. He jilted her, right at the last minute," said Teresa, with a proud stance, head in the air, and no tears at all. She had taken her volume from a ten to about a three, and she was suddenly perfectly calm., but you could tell she was still seething. That was even scarier, but before we knew it, we all did what only friends could do. We looked at each other in amazement and said in unison, "WHAT!"

"Jilted?" Dot asked, and you could see the wheels of inquisition turning.

Not one of us said a word for about a solid minute, then the questions came, one right after the other. They flowed like the waterfall of tears Teresa had cascading down her cheeks just seconds earlier.

"What exactly happened?" said Jackie.

"I can see why you're so upset," said Dot in a slightly patronizing but sincere way. "How's your sister taking it? I bet she's been crying harder than you? "

Teresa took a seat as if it was time for high tea, wiping her face and waving her hands around in dramatic Teresa fashion. She took a deep breath and announced, "Let me slow down so I can tell you everything."

All of us gathered as close to her as we could, not wanting to miss one juicy detail about this.

"When Sissy first met Fred, I knew it was a mistake," Teresa said confidently. "People think you don't know anything until you go to college, but I knew something was wrong. I mean, first of all, who names their child Fred? Not Frederick but Fred. And who wants to be with someone named Fred?" she explained, shrugging her shoulders in distaste.

"I don't know," Dot said with excitement, "But I've got an uncle named Fred, and he is the coolest. Everybody loves him."

I managed to give her a look before she could say anything else and further put her foot, not just in her mouth, but down her throat. I don't think Teresa even heard her, thank goodness. Teresa had a way of dismissing you, and once you were dismissed in her mind, you didn't exist anymore. Dot was lucky for right now.

"Hey Teresa," I asked, "Since you didn't like him anyway, were you surprised that he called it off?"

I thought that would be enough to move the story along. No such luck. It became painfully obvious that Teresa was going to drag this story out and get as much attention as she could for herself. She proceeded to give us the lengthy details, the agony she suffered overhearing the argument, the pain she felt (for her sister, of course), blah, blah, blah… Then she finally answered me.

"Yes, Pat," she addressed me, "I was surprised, but more than anything, I didn't want my Sissy to be hurt…. Not like that." Teresa delivered those words in a way that was soft and empathetic. Something was changing, and none of us understood what it was until much later.

While Teresa continued giving her account, I understood it was like being on a local train starting and stopping, seemingly going nowhere fast, and we were stuck trying to make sense of it all.

I had mentally stepped away from the conversation, contemplating how many happy endings Amy Porter had given us in her romance novels. None of them ever alluded to the possibility that someone would be jilted. There were illnesses and miracles; people even moved away, but they usually found their paths crossing later in the story, where love was rekindled. There was also an occasional breakup that was for the better, while new love came on the horizon. But intentionally calling off a wedding? Never!

"Pat, PAT," Dot called to me.

I turned to look in her direction. It took me a moment to even realize she had been calling my name. I guess my clueless expression said it all.

"I said, what do you think?" Dot repeated.

"What do I think about what?" I asked. Answering a question with a question was never allowed. My lack of attention to the matter was so obvious, I had to change my posture and get back in the game. I sat up and gave a look that expressed that I was more interested than I really was. Dot didn't seem to notice, so she continued the brief interrogation.

"Do you think Brenda should take him back?"

"Not in a million years," I said with great conviction.

"What if he came on bended knee, with a new, big ring, and apologized, and said he didn't mean it. What then?" Dot said with a deep exhale. She had exhausted herself.

This was a no-brainer for me. I responded with confidence. "Then I'd say no, no, no, and no. Case closed. End of story."

Dot then turned to Jackie to see if she could get a better response from her.

"Jackie, what would you do? I mean if you were in Brenda's shoes." An eternal optimist, Dot couldn't let it go. She needed happiness to be there for some reason.

"That's a hard question to answer," Jackie said. "I guess I'd pray about it first."

I didn't think we could roll our eyes simultaneously, but we did, and Jackie could have cared less. She went right ahead. "There is probably much more going on than we know about, so it would be hard to give an answer that would be the right one."

Dot didn't want the "right" answer or the God answer. Right then, she just wanted someone to give any answer that would allow her to get everything to where she thought it should be. She wanted everyone to be happy, and that meant love... romantic love, weddings and yes, happily-ever-after.

As Dot and Jackie went back and forth, I turned my attention to Teresa. She had moved over to the window and was staring out, lost in her own thoughts. For me, there was something unsettling about how quiet she'd become. Teresa was never this quiet. She always had an opinion, always had something to say, or maybe I should say, someone to talk and laugh about. I had never seen this side of her. I mustered up enough courage to have my own moment with her.

"Teresa..." I moved into her space at the window. "What's really happening with you?" I was treading in territory not visited too often. Teresa always seemed so much older than us; she seemed to have it all together, all the time. And there were times she was always willing to share things with me she didn't share with everybody, so I thought I was safe.

"What do you mean, Pat?" Teresa was almost whimpering as tears quietly streamed down her face.

"I know this is hard for you," I said, "I know you've let us in on a lot, but I can tell there's more to the story than just no wedding."

She took a breath and told me about how much her sister really wanted to be married.

"Brenda never saw the guys she met as friends or even just boyfriends. She was always looking for a potential husband. It didn't matter what anyone said, even me," she said with this distant look. Apparently, the Fred she saw her sister with was cruel, demeaning, and emotionally abusive. But she didn't describe him in those words. It wasn't until much later we could give him the 'Abuser' title because we didn't know how to define it back then.

She was telling me how Brenda was handling it, and out of nowhere, Teresa made a statement that would shape her thinking about men and how she would handle relationships from that day forward. The anger returned as she deliberately delivered each word: "I … will … never … let … a … man … do … that … to … me!"

Jackie and Dot interrupted our conversation with their own list of what's-going-to-happen-now questions.

"How is Brenda going to tell all those people who were planning to come?" Dot wanted to know, "And how many people are you going to have to tell? Will you have to pay for all that extra stuff? You know catering and all?" I was convinced Dot was not breathing through her words. "Your Mom and Dad must be as mad as Brenda, I'm sure they're out a lot of money…. Not to mention…." Her words trailed off, and she became quiet.

"Not to mention what?" Teresa asked.

Dot was speechless. She knew in her ramblings she had gone one step too far, and she needed help to get out of this one

"Not to mention what?" Teresa asked with a sharper tone.

I had to save Dot, but how?

Then it happened, a miracle: my mom saved the day. My mother entered the room, "Hey girls. Dot, your mom's outside. She needs you to hurry, she's got to take your cousin home."

"Yes, ma'am," Dot said with relief and sheer joy. "Bye ya'll."

I heard her speak, but I never saw her go. She was standing there one minute and the next she was opening the door to the car.

Everything changed after that day. It seemed our little book club took a turn, and we all went on to different things. Time passed, and we'd get together at my house for pizza every now and then, but not like we used to. The next thing we knew, we were getting ready for graduation from Carver High School and doing what most of our friends were doing: talking about prom; looking for a dress for prom; looking for a date for prom, blah, blah, blah…

I remember the last time Dot came by the house. Jackie was already there, and we were talking about what we wanted to do with the rest of our lives—after prom, of course. Jackie was all set. She met a hot guy named Grant who had transferred in mid-semester from Virginia. Grant's dad was black, and his mom was from Puerto Rico, and he was gorgeous. They had been an item ever since he got there, and Jackie was happier than I'd ever seen her. Dot, on the other hand, was unsettled, all over the place, and the closer we got to prom, the crazier she became.

But this day was a little different. We started talking about long-term plans. Our longest conversations were usually about make-up and clothes, but this night was different. We were looking through one of the fashion magazines and reading a short story called, 'Worth the Wait.' Dot became engrossed in it. Suddenly, she tossed the magazine and exclaimed, "Trash!" We were shocked, but that was only the first jolt.

"Dot," I said, "What in the world is wrong with you?"

Jackie crossed the room to pick up the magazine. "Just because you don't like the short story in this issue doesn't mean you have to tear the thing up," she said.

I took the magazine out of Jackie's hand as she crossed in front of me. I quickly looked at the synopsis of the story. The hero had returned from the military. His 'girl' heard he had been killed but wasn't willing to give up hope that he'd return, even though she hadn't heard from him for months. One day she went to the mailbox, and her whole life changed with a letter from him. It sounded typical of the stuff we used to read all the time.

"This looks pretty interesting to me. You were always up for a love story, Dot. What happened?" I asked.

"I guess I finally grew up," said Dot sadly. "All that happily-ever-after BS is for the birds. People aren't like that in real life. No one finds love, no one waits, no one really cares. One lie after another lie. I won't ever get on that…that *Love Train*. What a joke."

Jackie said, "So you're no longer pro-love? I remember we spent an entire day reading YOUR favorite books, and that's all they were about."

"I know," I agreed with Jackie. "All those hours daydreaming and hoping for my knight-in-shining-armor, and now you tell me he's not coming? Are you kidding me?" I said, tongue-in-cheek. Jackie and I laughed and gave each other a high five. But Dot wasn't laughing.

"Dot, you remember your favorite story was 'The Train To Forever'?" I asked.

"What about it?" said Dot.

"You loved everything about that book. You always said it had everything: handsome man, hopelessly in love with the plain Jane who thought that life had passed her by. Remember how all kinds of stuff got in the way of their relationship, but somehow, they ended up together? They met on the train and reunited on the train. Lots of stuff went on, but the little town they were headed to was called 'Forever.' Even more romantic. You always said if you could make it there, to 'Forever,' you'd live happily-ever-after. That's what you wanted."

"Humph. Those kinds of places don't exist. Those people don't exist."

"Where is all of this coming from, Dot?" Jackie asked.

Dot never really answered the question. In fact, that was the one and only time she seemed to have dismissed her dreams of romance on that level. I could sense our times together were coming to a close. Things were changing. We were not just growing up; we were growing apart. I think we all felt it and had silently, subconsciously, decided it was okay to move on. Eventually, our conversation returned to plans for the future, knowing that particular day had become a significant time in our past.

Back in the present, I cleaned up my snack and laid down for the night, peacefully reflecting on one last thing. It's funny when I think about it now, how my childhood friends crossed paths with my post-teen friends from time to time. There was always some occasion where we would see one another, but it was rarely all seven of us for any length of time. This wedding would be the first time in ages that we would all be together. Maybe Jean was right; maybe friendship with me was all we really had in common. While I was fine with that now, it wasn't entirely accurate, based on the wedding invitations. Bride-to-be Samantha had managed to maintain a relationship with each one of us. I smiled as I settled down for the night. Tomorrow would begin an interesting weekend.

CHAPTER 3
All Aboard

"All Aboard!"

Oh, how I loved that sound. I enjoyed being in the train station even when I wasn't traveling. This conductor had a no-nonsense, base voice that let the potential passengers know they had better get a move on.

"All Aboard!" he said again. I began to think about how many times I had heard those two words and rushed to get to the train with my mom just before they removed the three steps so that we could board. Sometimes I felt like that was as much fun as the trip itself. I began to think about what those train rides meant to me. There were a few short trips to see family, others for vacation, and of course, those that took me back-and-forth to college.

As I walked briskly in the opposite direction from the trains, I caught my reflection in the huge mirror facing the entryway.

"Not bad," I thought as I let out a deep sigh. A smile of contentment began to form across my flawless face. That's right, I said it: flawless face. "That Jean," I chuckled to myself. Her last journey of self-discovery put everyone on notice to improve their self-image. Since Jean had become an ATB (All Things Beautiful)

Consultant, she insisted that neither one of us should be seen without our make-up impeccably applied. As Jean would say, her tone crisp. "Well now, Ms. Patrice Williams-Hawthorne, you never know when you will meet 'The One.'"

And I would haughtily reply, "Of course, you're correct, Ms. Jeannette Alston-Miller. The market is always open," and we would say in unison as if perfectly rehearsed, "And somebody is always shopping." Then we'd start giggling like twelve-year-old's.

Jean's explanation of 'The One' should have been 'The Four,' after two marriages (one ending in divorce, the other one in a tragic ski accident), one broken engagement (turns out he was already married), and one whose fashion sense had much deeper meaning than anyone ever dreamed. It turns out his 'respect' for her was covering up a different kind of gender reveal.

At that point, we would both laugh hysterically and then reminisce about old times. Jean used to look for love all the time. Granted, she was looking in all the wrong places, but still looking. After her failed attempts though and the unsuccessful efforts of most of our friends to have that 'death do us part' experience, she'd become a little cynical about the journey and the outcome.

Eventually, Jeannette became Jean, and I became Pat. We became best friends and have been for over twenty-five years. It's funny how you can be in the same place, yet your paths never cross. We actually grew up a few miles apart but didn't meet until we went to college. We were inseparable; we shared so much. Some stories we didn't mind disclosing, having the freedom of transparency and real truth. Other life lessons we would take to the grave; we both knew it, and we were satisfied. That's what best friends do, after all. The interesting thing was, we were as opposite as two people could be. I was more laid back, reflective, cautious, and calm, while Jean had an insatiable appetite for life, a flirtatious nature, and was willing to throw caution to the wind and see where it would take her. But one thing was not a mystery: we were forever friends, always there for each other, no matter what.

When we lived in different cities due to our careers (I chose entertainment law while Jean chose Wall Street), we kept our lives on track and intact via all things electronic. However, there was no substitute for getting together face-to-face, and we'd look for any excuse to see each other. Samantha's wedding provided just that. I moved back home about two years ago after my divorce. Jean came back last year to sell the family home after her mom died but decided to stay. This was the first time we had actually seen each other in quite a while.

We decided to meet for lunch at the Crown Pavilion, which was located inside the recently renovated Imperial Train Station. It was a beautiful space and a great place to meet, greet and catch up on old times. I was enjoying the beauty of the moment when I heard…

"Well, hello there, flawless."

"No, it can't be," I said, turning slowly to see Jean walking towards me. I knew that low-toned, melodious voice, with a hint of southern drawl anywhere. Jean had that 'all eyes on me' kind of way about her. It always commanded attention, and that was fine with her.

"What do you mean it can't be?" Jean exclaimed as we rushed to give each other a huge, rocking-back-and-forth kind of hug. "Who else would it be?"

"Honey, I'm not talking about you being you," I said as Jean took the lead, going back to the table she had secured. "I'm talking about you being here before me." I couldn't help but get a slight dig in as I turned with the sincerest form of shock I could muster and gasped, holding my chest and looking her up and down, "Is everything all right? I mean, are you okay? You're not sick, are you?"

Jean looked at me with a concerned, confused, questioning stare.

"I haven't known you to be on time for anything a day in your life," I continued. "Not classes in school, not planes for vacations…shoot, you weren't even on time for your own wedding."

"I was too," Jean replied in her offended aristocratic voice. "At least I was for one of them…I think…maybe…maybe not. But that's old news." And then we doubled over laughing as we took our seats. The day had officially begun.

"Okay, so whose idea was it to take the train to this wedding anyway?"

We pointed to each other and, at the same time, said, "Yours."

"You've got that wrong, Sista," Jean stated. "It had to be you, Pat."

"Why?" I queried.

"Because I don't think in terms of 'ground transportation.' You know that," Jean said in her usual matter-of-fact manner.

As I started thinking back, it dawned on me how the arrangements came about.

"You just might be right, Jean," I responded.

"See, I told you."

"Actually, I don't think it was either of us. Remember, it was the last time we got together with Charlotte and Diamond?"

"Sort of," said Jean, who was much more interested in ordering a glass of wine than she was in getting an answer to how this all came about, even though she asked the question.

"That was almost a year ago. We had all received wedding invitations to the nuptials of Samantha Greene and Joshua Brown, and we laughed about the whole Crayola thing: Mrs. Samantha Greene-Brown." I couldn't stop laughing as I wrote the names in the air.

"Oh yeah, yeah, yeah, that was a hoot," Jean chuckled.

"Charlotte said we should get together today for lunch, meet in the morning and all take the train." It was all coming back to me now.

"Since when did we ever listen to what feather-brained Charlotte had to say?" quizzed Jean.

"Look," I said sternly, "We are not doing that this weekend." I was trying as hard as I could not to laugh. Charlotte was a bit of a scatterbrain, especially when it came to men.

"I think she has been engaged more than all of us put together, and she still has not made it down the aisle," said Jean with a sarcastic air of concern.

"Stop it, Jean." I attempted to reprimand her, knowing it was absolutely useless.

"Well, it's true."

I had to try and come to Charlotte's defense.

"She is just trusting, that's all."

"… and desperate. Remember the race car driver?" Jean said, determined to prove her point.

I gave her an expression that showed my memory wasn't as clear as hers.

"Come on, Pat, you remember. He was always telling her he was going off to race in one place or another. He said he was on the Nascar circuit, and she was way too 'fine' to be around those other drivers. Whenever he disappeared, it was because he had to compete. Every time she invited him somewhere, he was a no-show. Then she found out that not only was he NOT racing, he didn't even have a driver's license. AND he had another woman."

"Oh, that's right. How could I forget?" My memory was starting to return. "He didn't have a green card either, as I recall. He was one shady character."

"Easy on the eye," Jean commented, as she looked for the waiter, "But there wasn't an honest bone in his body. I feel bad for Charlotte sometimes."

"She always seems to choose the wrong guy."

"That's the point, Pat. She never 'chooses' anybody. Whoever comes along with just a little bit of game and a whole lot of charisma, she convinces herself he is the one and is ready to ride."

"I'd love to see her get herself together and stop trying to choose," I told Jean. "You know the word says—"

"Oh, here we go," Jean interrupted me before I could complete the sentence. "Where's the waiter? It's time to order something," she added as she raised her index finger to get his attention.

"No, now hear me out. The Word says, 'A man who findeth a wife, findeth a good thing.' Maybe if she concentrated on getting herself together, she wouldn't be so…well, desperate. And then she could really see the right man that God has for her," I said, but Jean was not paying me any attention.

"Well, look who's here," she said, pointing behind me. I turned around to see Charlotte. "Charlotte, my love," Jean continued, "We were just talking about you."

"Something good, I hope," said Charlotte excitedly with a huge smile on her face.

Before Jean could open her mouth again, I jumped in and, with a great deal of pure joy, assured her, "Of course it was. How could it be anything else?"

That was too close a call.

We greeted each other with hugs before Charlotte joined us at the table.

"I'm sorry I'm so late," Charlotte said, adjusting her too tight, too short, pencil skirt and bold print top with the deep V-neckline and making sure every strand of her weave was in place. She still had a great body, but time was knocking at the door, and Charlotte was determined not to answer. "You all know how it is when you've got a man that can't stand to let you out of his sight," she announced, grinning from ear to ear.

"No, we don't actually," Jean said under her breath as I gently kicked her under the table. She knew another diatribe was about to take shape and was trying to decide if she was up for it when I gave her that all too familiar 'be nice' look.

Charlotte took her compact out of her purse to make sure her make-up was just right. She made sure everything was in place before she cleared her throat and announced, "Ladies, I've got to make a quick call. Now don't talk about me while I'm gone," she said in her feather-light voice as she practically glided across the room.

"Oh, we wouldn't dare," said Jean with an insincere smile, tipping her glass in the air and following Charlotte's departure. She couldn't wait for her to leave the table.

CHAPTER 4
The More Things Change,
The More They Stay The Same

Before Jean could say a word, I advised her in my most intentional voice, "Jean, we've gone through this before."

Jean gave me a puzzled, what-are you-talking-about look, but I was not deterred.

"You know what I mean, Jean. We are going to have a great, drama-free weekend."

Jean settled back in her chair for a moment, then raised up and quietly leaned forward.

"I'll be nice, but I'm telling you something isn't right."

"How do you know?" I asked.

"I can just tell," Jean continued.

I didn't say another word. I picked up the menu and began to study it like I was searching the scriptures rather than looking for the Special of the Day. It didn't take Charlotte long to return, phone in hand with an unsettled look that rapidly turned from a disappointed smile to a wide grin. Maybe Jean was right.

"Did I miss anything?" Charlotte asked with a demure smile.

Before I could offer an answer, Jean spoke up.

"Charlotte, I've got to ask you something."

Uh oh, here we go, I thought.

Charlotte looked at her seriously as she put her napkin in her lap, and Jean continued.

"Why are you always late? Honey, you look like a million dollars, but if you got everything that together, you ought to be able to get somewhere on time," Jean said with a slightly sarcastic tone and laugh. "So, what kept you?"

"Well, you know, or maybe you don't," Charlotte said, giving the sarcasm right back with a 'helpless-little-me' tone thrown in for good measure. "But when a man thinks the sun rises and sets on you. it's hard to tear yourself away."

I immediately responded, "We know exactly what you mean. When your boo is into you, he is into you, isn't that right, Jean?"

"Absolutely! And they want to do everything for you, and I do mean everything," Jean said playfully.

Charlotte looked back and forth between Jean and me, studying our faces. She decided to dive right in. Apparently, she felt she needed to do some catching up and fast.

"I had no idea that each of you ladies had someone special in your life," she began excitedly.

Neither Jean nor I said a word. I sipped my lemon water, and Jean stirred her tea slowly and deliberately. We both began studying the room as if looking for someone.

Charlotte began looking around as well, waited about ten seconds, which was as long as she could contain herself, and exclaimed, "Come on now, tell me about these men you've been seeing."

Jean and I looked at each other, and Jean spoke first, asking very seriously, "What men? Is there a man in your life, Pat?"

I raised my shoulders in a clueless way saying, "What are you talking about? There's no man in my life."

Before Jean could say another word, Charlotte spoke up, "You two just told me—"

"Told you what, exactly," Jean said, narrowing her eyes as if she was totally confused by what Charlotte was suggesting.

I couldn't take it any longer. I erupted into laughter, and Jean followed. We were falling over in our seats.

"Charlotte, you should see the look on your face. Oh, this is priceless," Jean said as we tried, unsuccessfully, to pull it together. It seemed the two of us were the only ones enjoying the little joke though. Charlotte wasn't as amused, at least not at first, but she gradually came around. The three of us tried our best not to disturb the other patrons, but we laughed till we cried.

"Okay, that's enough," Charlotte said, dabbing at her make-up with a tissue she found in her purse. "That was a good one. I admit you had me there for a minute." She continued laughing. "I mean, I should have known better." Her laugh was not contagious. Those few words sucked the air right of the room, and it didn't take long for her to realize she was laughing alone.

"So are you suggesting that I couldn't have a man in my life," said an offended Jean.

"Oh, come on now, you two," I jumped in, trying to keep things calm and lighthearted. I could sense things rapidly spiraling downhill. "We all had a good laugh. Let's not get all deep now."

The thought of how giddy Charlotte could get over even a conversation about men was too funny as far as I was concerned. When I pointed that out, the laughter easily returned to the table, and we all realized how ridiculous the situation was. Definitely nothing to be offended about. One thing it did for sure was open the door for Charlotte to do what she loved doing, which was talk about her love life.

Before Jean and I could ask Charlotte about her current romantic adventures, Charlotte raised her hand into the air, wiggling her fingers like each one was having a dance party. She settled down and kept her hand still long enough to expose a huge, jaw-dropping diamond ring!

Jean was the first to speak, and her first word was, "WOW!" Then she just stared.

Charlotte was almost hysterical, describing the ring and the proposal. Not one word about the man until I inquired, and then she searched in her purse, quickly showing us a picture and looking at it herself with wide-eyed devotion.

Jean was still staring at the ring in awe.

All I had to add to the moment was, "Close your mouth, Jean. Breathe, Jean. Earth to Jean!"

Jean followed orders, closed her mouth like she'd been shot, and pursed her lips together tightly. She asked Charlotte to see the picture of her intended again and then quickly turned her gaze back to the humongous ring.

"That's one reason why I wanted to come today," said Charlotte, beaming from ear to ear. "I wanted to see you in person and tell you all the good news." And then she did it. She made the big announcement: "I'm getting married in six months!

We were stunned.

"Charlotte, who is this man? I mean, really, and how long have you known him? Have you even known him for six months?" I couldn't misconstrue the fact that Jean was genuinely concerned when she asked her question.

"Not long," Charlotte said as she looked at her hand proudly. You could tell she didn't like Jean asking the question.

"How long, Charlotte?" Jean pressed.

"Not long, but what does it matter? I know it seems soon, but when you know, you just know," replied Charlotte. Her guard was coming up, and clearly, I seemed to be the only one that noticed. "Don't spoil it for me, guys. I wanted my two best friends to be the first to know so you'd share this with me." She extended her hand to take the picture back, brushed her fingers across it with this breathless stare, and returned it to her purse.

Jean turned her head slightly to the side, held her napkin to her face as if wiping her mouth, and whispered to me, "Did she just say her two best friends. Are we her best friends? Really?"

The only thing I could do was say (rather softly), "I guess." I was as confused as Jean on that one.

"Charlotte, we're just concerned about you," I told her.

"No," said Charlotte like a defiant child, "You're just jealous."

Jean replied with fire. "Trust me, honey; that is NOT the case."

"Okay, ladies, simmer down," I said. I felt I had to reel this in somehow, but Charlotte was on a roll.

"Why can't you just be happy for me?" Charlotte was tearing up, and that was never a good sign.

"Charlotte, we want to see you happy, more than you probably realize," Jean said. "But, I mean, I bet you haven't known this man ninety days, and that's important. Tell her, Pat, tell her about your ninety-day rule."

"Jean, this is not the time," I said.

"No, Pat, this is the perfect time," she insisted.

Charlotte gave me an expectant look, so I began my little spiel, speaking slowly and deliberately. "Charlotte, you know they always say when you first meet a person, you don't really meet them, you meet their representative. Best foot forward and all that. Well, I believe that if you're with someone and they're not showing you who they really are, they can only hold up the façade for about ninety days, and somewhere in that time, if there's deception, you're going to see it. The signs will be there."

Charlotte's eyes started to brim with tears, and in her most composed way, she said, "Please, excuse me, ladies. I have to go to the little girls' room. I'll be right back." Then she got up and left.

"Now look what you've done, Jean. She won't be right for the rest of the afternoon," I said.

"ME!" Jean exclaimed.

"Yes, you. I don't see anyone else sitting here," I replied. Jean looked at me shocked, although I didn't understand why, so I thought I'd help her out.

"You know how Charlotte is. She can't stand too many questions about her latest and greatest, especially when she doesn't want to or can't really answer them."

I spoke as firmly as I could without elevating my voice too much. I didn't want an argument with Jean, and I hated to see Charlotte's feelings hurt. I also hated to see her make another mistake: a ring and a wedding in what sounded like less than six months. And whenever Charlotte's defensive attitude started coming through it was a clear indicator, deep down inside, that she sensed something wasn't right, just like we did.

"Okay, Pat, maybe I was a little harsh, but I hate to see her go through this again. I really do. This has disaster written all over it. I want Charlotte to know she's not some pathetic trick who'll fall for anything. Did you really look at the picture? There's something about him. Whoever this guy is, he's probably lying through his teeth because he knows he can. He's probably sitting somewhere laughing with his buddies over a beer at how gullible she is. We're her friends, and we ought to speak up and help her see the light."

The more agitated Jean became, the calmer I became. Funny how that worked.

"Jean," I called her name quietly but with the intention to begin the settling down process. I wanted Jean to be in a good space when Charlotte returned.

"Okay, I hear what you're saying, and it's not that I totally disagree with you, but you have to take everything into consideration. This is Charlotte we're talking about. She does this all the time. Forever hopeful that this is THE ONE. And besides, did she ask for our opinion? No. She just wants to be happy, even if it's short-lived. I'd rather be happy for her today, so I can be there for her tomorrow because these antics are getting more and more difficult for her to recover from."

Jean took a deep sigh and nodded in agreement.

"One last thing, I think you're dead wrong about Mr. Mystery Man, lying, laughing, and having a beer with his buddies." Jean was getting ready to cut me off, but I quickly continued. "If that ring is real, he's drinking something a lot more expensive than beer." We both looked at each other and began to laugh at my feeble attempt at humor.

"Okay, you two. What did I miss?"

And with those few words, Charlotte took her seat at the table, wearing a smile that said, 'No matter what, all is well… at least for now.'

I gave Charlotte a knowing smile and reached over to pat her on the shoulder.

Jean sheepishly said, "Charlotte, look, I want to—"

Charlotte didn't let her finish. She gently shook her head, no, and just remained, well, Charlotte. She took out her compact, dabbed at her make-up, lifted her eyes, and looked over the small mirror with a sincere 'Charlotte smile', which was her acknowledgment that she accepted the apology she was sure Jean was about to offer … and she was right. We all looked at each other in a way that settled the issue. We knew the pattern, and like it or not, we had agreed to accept each other, warts and all, many years before this latest fiasco.

Charlotte broke the silence. "Have you ordered anything, Pat?"

"I haven't. But all of a sudden, I am starving. Jean, what did you get?"

"Right now, I'd settle for a menu," she replied, and with that, we all began to laugh again. Jean called the waiter over, and he gave us menus while sharing the specials with precision. It didn't take a minute for us to place our orders and watch Jean follow his every step as he left our table.

"Why Jean," Charlotte mused. "You should be ashamed of yourself."

"Why Charlotte?" Jean said with a twinkle in her eye, mimicking Charlotte's tone, "One should never have to apologize for appreciating the view of one's surround-dings."

"As long as one doesn't embarrass oneself or one's friends in the process," I said. Jean and Charlotte looked at each other and back at me. They had settled on something. My attempt to mimic the two of them was an epic failure, but it sure kept the mood at the table light, and that's what was needed in that moment.

Jean spoke first. She gave me a look of compassion and said, "Girl, now that was just sad."

Before anyone could respond, we all heard the vibration of a cell phone. As each of us searched to see whose phone it was, we realized we had all received a group text from Diamond stating she had just parked the car and was on her way. She had sent a text yesterday though saying she wasn't going to be able to make it.

"I wonder what happened?" I inquired, hoping someone at the table knew.

"Doesn't really matter," said Charlotte. "I'm always glad to see my Diamond." She looked admiringly at the rock on her finger without even realizing that she was striking up a conversation with her left hand.

With a gesture of agreement, Jean added, "I'll be glad to see her as well because I think the two of you"—pointing to Charlotte and myself—"were responsible for this lunch and train ride, and I don't have any details. This is a very special weekend. After all, we are going to witness the demise…I mean, celebration of our dear friends, Samantha and Joshua." She raised her glass, and Charlotte and I followed suit. "A toast to the happy couple."

Jean was the first one to see Diamond approach the table.

"Well, if this is what being a stay-at-home mom looks like, I'm about to make some changes in my life for real. Honey, you look absolutely fabulous," Jean said in her most complimentary tone.

Charlotte squealed when she saw Diamond as if she finally had an ally in this destination marriage.

"Diamond, you look amazing," I said in agreement. She had lost weight and was absolutely glowing. "I don't think I've ever seen you looking so good. You're radiant."

"Well, thank you," Diamond said, blushing just a little.

"The last time we saw you, you were talking about bottles and baby fat, but no more baby fat for you, Miss Lady. What did you do?" asked Jean.

"She got a personal trainer," Charlotte quickly interjected, "And he is some kind of fine."

Jean immediately leaned across the table and said, "Now you've whetted my appetite for the full scoop. And look at you, turning a true shade of lobster red. There is a story here ladies, no holds barred," said Jean as she motioned for the waiter to bring another menu. "C'mon, spill the beans."

I'm not usually one to engage in gossip; however, if the person is talking about himself/herself, it doesn't meet the criteria of gossip, unless you share it with someone else. I decided I didn't care. Whatever it was, I wanted to know.

"Weren't you going to the gym at one point?" I asked.

"Yes, I was—"

"Is that where you met this trainer?" I thought I'd jump right in.

"Well, sort of—"

"What's that mean, sort of? Either you did, or you didn't," Jean said, getting frustrated, "How do you sort of meet somebody?" She obviously wanted this train of thought moving along faster. "And how does hubby feel about the trainer and the transformation?"

"Will you give her a chance to answer one question before you fire off another one?" Charlotte said. She then turned her attention to Diamond and reassuringly said, "Continue, and take it slow so you won't miss sharing not one little bit." She emphasized the last three words saying them as seductively as she could. We all laughed.

"Okay, ya'll, that's enough," Diamond said. "There's really nothing to tell. You know how I was struggling to get the weight off once I had Macy. I had tried diets, I was exercising. I'd talked to a couple of friends and joined some groups that talked about nutrition and stuff. Have you all heard about the whole Keto thing?"

As Charlotte and I prepared to respond, Jean jumped in, unable to stand the suspense another minute. She narrowed her eyes and told Charlotte, "Get to the good stuff. We don't care about the exercise and diet options; we just want to know about the trainer. What's his name anyway?"

"His name is Rashaad," Diamond said, "But I just call him Ray." Everyone at the table detected a change in her voice when she said his name.

Uh oh, I thought. There might be something more happening on this little passenger train than any of us thought.

"Soooo, how did 'Ray' come into the picture?" Jean asked. "How long have you been seeing him…uh training with him, and how often?"

Jean was firing questions like a locomotive picking up speed.

"Jean," I said, "Give her time to think…I mean, breathe…I really mean, think and breathe."

Diamond shook her head. The waiter returned, and she ordered a lemonade. Jean grinned and said, "You know how I like to solve mysteries, and this one is going to be great. So out with it. Details, please."

Diamond began, removing any air of mystery, "I really hate to disappoint you, but there isn't much to tell. I was going to the gym but couldn't seem to get consistent. I had the machines. The classes were okay, but it just wasn't working for me. Well, hubby found a place that had couples' classes, and we signed up. We were both having fun, but the weight wasn't coming off quickly enough. Someone suggested a personal trainer and recommended Ray, and there you have it. Mystery solved."

Jean couldn't hide her disappointment.

Diamond couldn't help but laugh at Jean's disappointment.

"Couples indeed," Jean said, "Why didn't you say this was a 'me-and-my hubby' plan."

"You didn't give me a chance," laughed Diamond. "Besides, you know how committed I am to my husband and to God. I'd never enter into anything outside of my marriage."

"Not even a little ole flirtatious fling?" asked Jean.

"Not even, and not ever," whispered Diamond with a look of sheer contentment.

I had to admit, the thought of our little stay-at-home mom having a daytime strangers-on-a-train adventure to share would have spiced up the afternoon. I was surely not looking for a couples-sweating-in-the-sauna-together thing. But it was nice to know she, hubby, God, and family were all in their rightful place. Things were fine and drama-free.

As everyone chatted away and caught up with each other, I looked at the table and smiled at how my three friends from the days of my youth (so to speak) were so much like my three friends from college and beyond. Everybody with travel plans, on their own journey, boarding different trains, taking different paths depending on their age and stage in life. Teresa was a lot like Jean in many ways, always appearing to have things under control, always unapologetic, always finding humor in the situation, even if it was a little 'cutting." They were able to be passengers on any train at any given time: different career paths, different destinations, people popping in and out of their lives. Life was truly a journey for them, an awaiting adventure. It was always all good as long as they could visit the club car from time to time, enjoy who they met, and leave at any moment.

Charlotte and Dot were a lot alike. And while they came from different places (Charlotte was raised by a single mom with substance abuse issues; Dot a workaholic dad and soccer mom), they always looked for the happily-ever-after. They both believed that the answer to everything was someone to rescue them from…well, whatever. They had the knight-in-shining-armor in mind, but they kept traveling the same path—the *Commuter Train* mentality. Commuter passengers are pretty much the same: they start in one place and ultimately end in the same space. No deviation. No adventure. Simply going from one place to another, or rather one relationship to another. They're not always sure what they're looking for, but they go with some kind of plan all mapped out, determined to find someone to fit the pattern they've put in place. The Charlotte's and Dot's of the world are usually on the *Romance* and *Commitment Trains*.

Then there's Jackie and Diamond. Solid citizens. Always using wisdom even early on, looking for the best. Always able to see the good, the bad, and the ugly; and adjust accordingly. They were also the ones with a God message of good and evil and hope and love. From the time we were kids until we gained some semblance of maturity, God always had a place and made His presence known through them. I think they could easily be my conductors.

Now there is one other train we haven't mentioned, and those who board are not always easy to identify. Their relationships begin and end fairly quickly, but they are none the worse for wear. They always land on their feet looking like they just dodged a bullet. If they are fortunate to find someone who is willing to help carry the weight, they are too suspicious to allow them to come alongside and love them. They can't go into the future because they are so busy explaining, protecting themselves from the past, and holding everyone accountable for it. Determined no one will take advantage of them. They never totally let go of the reasons why they were hurt or own their part in the train going off track. I think they resemble the passengers who end up on the *Freight Train*, carrying baggage and lots of it. Not able to let go of what happened before, yet always wanting more. And when they are in a place to move forward somehow, they manage to self-sabotage. That would be Samantha Greene!

CHAPTER 5
Enter The Bride To Be

Samantha and I had been friends forever, the kind of friends who could pick up where we left off regardless of how much time we'd spent apart. Samantha's parents were older and very strict, so she didn't get to do much when we were growing up. For some reason, her parents liked me, and I became Samantha's door to the outside world. That meant whatever I got to do, Samantha got to do; whoever I knew, Samantha knew, including my three buddies from back in the day. Samantha was a sweetheart, not a mean bone in her body. She was the kind of person you just wanted to see happy. She wanted to get on that *Romance Train* and end up at the last station with nothing but joy and the right man to share her life with. It just didn't seem to be in the cards for her, though. Something always seemed to happen to her happily-ever-after.

I don't remember how much time had passed but I ran into Samantha quite unexpectedly last spring, right after she announced she was getting married. We both found ourselves at a university event and agreed to meet for dinner. Samantha picked the restaurant, and I was glad she did. It was a quiet, little bistro, perfect for food and conversation. As usual, I was the first to arrive, but the wait was short. I wasn't there five minutes before Samantha appeared. Heads always turned when she entered a room, whether she was in running gear with a free-flowing natural do; or an updo and regal attire fit for a White House gala. Today she had chosen a pin-striped boyfriend shirt with gray slacks, amazing jewelry, and the kind of make-up that didn't make her look 'made-up.' Something was off, though; I could feel it.

"Hey Samantha," I said excitedly as she approached our table.

"Hi Pat," she replied. "I hope I didn't keep you waiting."

Samantha had that kid-in-a-candy-store, wide-eyed look she always had when she was happy.

We hugged when we greeted each other, just like always. It was so good to see her.

"You didn't keep me waiting at all," I assured her. "I just got here."

We took our seats and sat there like excited kids for a few minutes, starting our sentences at the same time, then stopping to giggle like schoolgirls.

"Okay, you go first," I said to Samantha.

"No, you," she said as her laughter began to settle.

"Okay, okay," I agreed with resignation, too happy to see my friend to debate about it. "I don't really know where to start, so let's just do the obvious. Girl, how are you doing, and what have you been up to?"

"Actually, quite well. I absolutely adore my job," Samantha was obviously happy to report. She looked like she was making an announcement that sealed a huge real estate deal. She was absolutely radiant. But still...

"What are you doing now?" I asked. It had been a while since we last saw each other, and Samantha had a way of changing career paths like other people changed shoes. She wasn't flighty or anything; she just knew how to weigh opportunities and make wise choices.

It was an easy conversation. Samantha and I always seemed to be able to talk as if we had seen each other the day before. We reminisced for quite a while over a simple but tasty, late-day meal. As we waited for dessert, Samantha spoke up.

"I am so glad I ran into you. I've been meaning to call you for quite some time," she said.

I nodded in agreement. "I know. We do this all the time—promise to keep in touch, but never seem to be able to with our schedules and all."

As we continued to talk, an uneasy feeling began to well up inside of me. From time to time, Samantha's smile would fade, and she would just stare into space like she was doing now. I snapped my fingers, tilted my head, looked deeply into her vacant stare, and asked in a soft but commanding voice, "Hey, Samantha, yoohoo." I snapped my fingers again. "Earth to Samantha."

She immediately refocused and said, "I'm sorry, Pat." Then it happened. The tears she had been holding back started to fall. She couldn't contain them any longer. "I've needed a friend to really talk to for so long. Someone who knows me well enough to let me be totally honest and transparent." She took a deep breath and continued. "Oh Pat, I'm just miserable, and I'm tired of pretending that I'm not. All I've wanted, ever since I can remember, is to just be happy. I'm tired of getting hurt. I'm tired of feeling lost. I'm tired of feeling lonely even when I'm with someone. I don't know whether I'm coming or going, and I don't know what to do about it."

"Samantha, what's going on?" I asked empathetically while searching through my purse. Where was a clean Kleenex tissue when you need one? I found a pack and handed it to Samantha. "Where's all this coming from? And why didn't you call me? You know you can talk to me, and it doesn't go anywhere. You know that."

"I know. I guess I was just embarrassed," said a sniffling Samantha as she tried to pull herself together.

"Embarrassed about what?"

"How I'm really feeling."

"Samantha, I would think this would be the happiest time of your life. You're getting married, and that's what you've always wanted. We've all saved the date, and we're looking forward to it," I responded, utterly confused.

"I know," said Samantha, and then quietly added, "I was too."

"Wait a minute, why are you talking past tense?"

I thought to myself, this is serious for real.

"Pat, I am terrified. One minute I want to call it off, the next minute, I want to elope because I just can't wait. My emotions are all over the place. I can't think straight. There's so much to do to get ready, the catering, flowers, guest lists. It's just making me sick."

"Are you sure you're not…?"

"Not what? "Samantha asked as she wiped her nose.

I just looked at her and raised my eyebrows.

Samantha's big brown eyes got even bigger as she realized what I was asking. "Are you crazy? Have you lost your mind? Good grief, Pat."

"Well, it's a fair question." At least I thought it was, but I didn't press the matter. I thought it was better to quickly move along. That train had definitely left the station. "Okay, since we've ruled that out, what else is going on? Are your parents okay? Are you stressed about something? Your health okay? Is it financial? Is it something about Joshua?"

Each question received a negative nod. If it wasn't family, stress, health, money, and her man wasn't gay, I was at a loss. I just couldn't figure out what had Samantha so discombobulated. We sat in silence for longer than was comfortable, and then Samantha dropped the bomb.

"Jeffrey." Staring into space, Samantha had finally said it. "It's Jeffery."

Oh yeah, this is serious, I thought. I had not heard that name in years, and with good reason. Jeffrey was the man of Samantha's dreams, or so she thought. So, we all thought, at first. He was attentive, charismatic, at home with all of her friends and family, knew just enough about any subject to be engaging in conversation, wasn't hurting financially, well-groomed, and fine. Did I say fine? Yes, I did! The two of them were considered 'the couple.' Jeffrey was indeed a catch. And thank God he was—caught, I mean. It seems like he wasn't just wanted by Samantha—he was wanted in at least three states for everything from fraud to assault and battery, Ponzi schemes, a string of DUI's, and I don't know what all else.

"What if I'm making the same mistake and I'm too trusting?" Samantha asked. "What if all this is moving too fast? What if I need to take a step back and really weigh all the pros and cons of going into marriage at all? What if…?"

"What if you put all those wedding jitters in a bag, zip it up, and never open it again?" I advised with authority. Case closed. Over. Done. I had spoken. "Listen, Samantha, you can't compare the two," I said with reassuring calm and wisdom. "Jeffrey was an accident waiting to happen, and you just didn't see it coming. None of us did. You looked at him through the lens of what he showed you, not who he really was or who he might be, one day, maybe. You hardly had a chance to get to know him. It seemed like you met, dated, got engaged, and were on the way to the altar in the same week."

"That's what I mean. I didn't know how to say 'no' and slow things down. I didn't want to wait. I thought I'd lose him if I did. I was caught up in something that got out of control, and I didn't know what to do. Maybe that's who I am, someone who just goes along and can't make a decision. I made so many excuses for Jeffrey when things started getting a little crazy. Am I doing the same with Joshua?"

"Are things getting a little crazy with him?" I asked, now on high alert. I waited but got crickets. "Well, are they?"

Samantha just sat there, silent and sad.

I started getting a little agitated. "Okay, Samantha, I'm going to ask you this once, and only once: is Joshua on the down-low?"

Samantha still didn't speak and was once again on the verge of tears, but her eyes were giving me a solid, 'Absolutely not.'

"I'll take that as a 'No.' Is he abusive...physically, mentally, I mean—"

Samantha cut me off.

"Stop, Pat. Just stop. It's none of those things." She wiped her eyes and sought to calm me down. "I mean, Joshua can be a little controlling sometimes, but it doesn't bother me and is nothing to be concerned about," she said in a very matter-of-fact tone.

Okay, now she was giving me a headache. I didn't want to think that hard, and I didn't know what to say. Was there something she wasn't being honest about? I thought she was really sure of their relationship this time. I didn't want to lead her into the wrong train of thought.

"Hear me out, Pat," Samantha said with a strange kind of halting resolve. "What if there is really something I'm not considering? I mean, I've known him for years, but we've, you know, dated on and off. Granted, Jeffrey and I hadn't known each other that long, but if I really want to be honest, there was always something that made me uneasy. I just didn't want to admit it."

"This is not that," I told her. "You've known Joshua for ages. The two of you were friends before you were anything else. You've taken it slowly. You've been engaged now for the short side of forever, and you are both ready to commit to a covenant relationship and not a ride on a *Runaway Train*. Think about it."

Samantha sat there, taking in everything I was saying. I didn't rush the process. I could see it on her face as she contemplated the things I was telling her. I could see a more relaxed countenance returning to a face that was tight with fear a few moments before.

"I guess you're right, Pat. Just pre-wedding jitters, I suppose."

"What do you mean, 'suppose I'm right?'" Of course, I'm right. Aren't I always?" I said, with a clutching-of-the-pearls look.

We both laughed, but I felt there was something unfinished about the discussion. Still, the rest of the afternoon was light-hearted as we talked about new horizons, old times, old friends. That's when our conversation got interesting.

"You will never guess who I saw not too long ago," Samantha offered.

"Okay, since I'll never guess, why don't you tell me?" I chided.

"Teresa!" Samantha announced.

"What? No. Teresa, no H Teresa? I haven't seen or heard anything about her since her mom died, and that was years ago. How is she doing?"

"I didn't get to talk to her. She was a speaker at a conference I was covering for a magazine." Samantha was an amazing freelance writer, which is part of the reason those who knew her well always called her by her full name. Sam Greene was her by-line which opened some doors for her early on because people assumed Sam was a guy. For some reason, the general public didn't give 'Samantha' as much credit and respect as they gave 'Sam,' but that too is another story for another day.

"What kind of conference was it? Religious? Political? Teresa was always involved in something that had to do with the community, whether it was working on feeding the hungry or helping people get housing."

I could tell by the look on Samantha's face that there might be a detail or two I was unaware of.

"Well, she is actually very community-minded, but it's not the hungry or homeless community. It's more colorful than that. She's part of the rainbow. You know, the LBGTQ community."

"Whoa," I said, caught off guard by that news, although I shouldn't have been. Something happened when Teresa's sister Brenda's wedding plans went down the tubes. I never quite understood it, but she wasn't the Teresa no H that I grew up with after that. I sat back and let Samantha fill in all the blanks.

"You remember when you told me about that fiasco with Teresa and her sister and all," Samantha began.

"Of course. No one could ever forget that," I recalled, "But none of us could figure out why Teresa was so upset about the wedding being called off. "

"There was a lot more, and I mean a lot more, to it than that," Samantha kept going. "It seems Brenda's fiancé called it off because he had slept with Teresa. He didn't realize how old, or I should say young, Teresa really was. It was a one-night stand, and the guilt was killing him. Plus, he could have gone to jail because Teresa was considered a minor at the time."

"Samantha, no!!" I exclaimed. "How is it I didn't know about any of this? Was I living under a rock somewhere?"

"There was a lot going on for all of us if you remember, Pat. It just wasn't something we thought about. Besides, Teresa always had so much drama going on, real and unreal, we couldn't add up the pieces. You and I hadn't become really tight yet, and as we got closer, I just assumed you knew and didn't want to bring it up."

"I do remember some of it," I said, thinking back. "It was that summer that we all went our separate ways. I came South to stay with my granny because she was sick. You went up North and stayed up there to go to school. And Teresa…" I paused for a bit… "Nobody knew where she went, but when she came back, she was mean as a rattlesnake. "How do you happen to know all this?" I asked Samantha.

"Well, her mom and my aunt were good friends. I always had big ears and my head in a book. No one ever thought I was paying attention to them, and I usually didn't. But they always talked loudly. I listened and learned."

All I could do was shake my head in silence.

"There was talk about her having a baby. It was unconfirmed. There was a lot of talk about a lot of things. That time seemed to be the crossroads for her. We've actually kept in touch, believe it or not, and I wanted to let you know before you saw her again. Whenever we talked, she would always ask about you. Running into you couldn't have happened at a better time. I invited her to the wedding, and she said she'd be there. I didn't want you to be surprised when you saw her. She doesn't look quite the same."

To say that brought us to a pregnant pause is an understatement. I was without words, and I gave a sigh of relief when Samantha broke the silence. But that relief was perhaps a little premature. Time to bring on the coffee.

CHAPTER 6
My Turn

"You know what, Pat," Samantha began. "In all the years I've known you, you never really talk about yourself. You're always the listening ear for everyone else, but I know things haven't always been peachy keen for you."

"How do you know?" I asked.

"Odds," said Samantha with a sheepish smile. "Odds are that everyone has valleys and mountains in their life. Besides, one of your favorite sayings is, 'Everyone has a story; it just depends on whether or not they are willing to tell it.' So, what's your story, Pat?"

Her question made me a little uneasy.

"I'm not very interesting," I told her. "There's not really very much of a story where I'm concerned."

I wasn't sure where she wanted that query to take her, but she was accurate in her assessment of me not sharing much. I was the listening ear for everyone, even as a kid. I think I'd been working in the club car of everybody else's train my whole life. It just seemed that the more I listened to what other people had to say, the less interested they became in listening to me. I'd answer questions if asked, but my days of volunteering information about myself had long passed. I had gotten used to keeping things about myself to myself. But it looked like I was caught this time, and for whatever reason, it was okay. I wanted to talk to Samantha.

"I'd have to think very hard to determine a time you were not in my life," I told Samantha, "So I guess I assumed you know everything about me."

"Not by a long shot. I didn't even know your real name was Patrice until we were about ten years old," she said with a side smile. We both had to chuckle because she was right. I guess there were some secrets to be shared, and I was willing to answer her questions, though not necessarily volunteer.

"I feel like I'm about to be interviewed for some kind of exposé," I said as I added cream and sugar to my coffee. The mood had definitely shifted.

"Not really, Pat. It's just that I'm finding people can be in our lives for all our lives, and we don't really know as much about them as we think. I have always looked up to you and admired how you handled your journey. Right now, since I need help stabilizing my own, I came for some advice and wisdom. So, how do you do it?"

"How do I do what?"

"Live without a relationship and not be bothered by it."

I couldn't help but laugh. "What makes you think I'm not bothered by it?"

Samantha gave me that 'Discovery-Channel-look' as if she was really onto something. I decided to continue before she could let her mind run amuck.

"It's simple, Samantha. I took what I thought was the safe, pain-free way out. I was always the friend, the one who gave advice, the level-headed one. That was the role

I played. I didn't always start there, but it seemed like that's where I ended up. I tried marriage, but it didn't work, so I came to the conclusion it wasn't for me, and that's that. End of story."

"End of story? I don't think so," said Samantha. "I knew you were married, and I knew you didn't stay married long, and you got divorced. Did you ever come close to marrying again?"

"Why are you asking me this stuff?" I asked, a little uneasy. "Are you trying to set me up with somebody? If you are, I'm not interested," I said emphatically.

"See, that's what I'm talking about. How do you know you're not interested? And before you answer, no, I'm not trying to set you up. You look like you might grab your purse and head for high ground," Samantha said. "I guess relationships have been taking up so much of my brainpower, and I realized it really isn't something we ever talked about. At least you have never talked about it, and I guess I'm just curious."

I sat trying to figure out how long I wanted to ride this train or if I even wanted to be a passenger. I didn't realize my love life held such intrigue for anyone else. Knowing my circle, if Samantha was curious, there must have been some discussion about my love life or lack thereof with some of the other members of my group of close 'friends.'

"Where would you like for me to begin? And don't say at the beginning." I was trying with everything in me to keep it light. Realistically, my take on romance and all that came with it was anything but light.

Samantha actually started. "For as long as I can remember, I wanted to grow up and get married. I wanted my husband and I to be a power couple with a beautiful home, a Tahoe, a Camry, and a couple of brilliant, well-behaved kids. I wanted a career, probably real estate. I wanted the flexibility to raise my kids and have a hot meal ready when hubby came home. And of course, I wanted amazing, jaw-dropping sex, often.

"How young were you when you were having these little fantasies of yours?" I asked.

"The sex part came way after the Barbie dream house," Samantha laughed. "But it was the picture I painted for a long time."

"Sounds like you were all-girl. No kickball for you, right? Tea parties and dress up all the way?"

I felt like Samantha wanted to talk as much about her story as she wanted to listen to mine. If I was careful and asked the right questions, I figured I could turn this whole thing around, and my story wouldn't have to be told. Fat chance, but I was hopeful until she said…

"What about you, Pat? I don't see you as the tom-boy type, and I don't think you were the guest at the tea party either. So, when did Prince Charming enter your thoughts and dreams?"

"I really didn't spend much time daydreaming. I had too much fun listening to everyone else's little dramas. I loved romantic movies though, and I believed, for a time, that Prince Charming was going to come along," I said with a long dramatic sigh. Samantha was becoming lost in the possibilities, so I figured I'd better bring reality back. Changing my posture and tone from wishful thinking to matter of fact, I continued. "That didn't last long. I didn't find a prince. I didn't even pass by a Prince-in-Training. I found one frog after another after another.

Then one day I heard a deep voice say, 'Can you tell me where the Pastor's study is?' I turned around and looked into the most beautiful, soft, hazel eyes, with hair I knew I wanted to run my fingers through, a toothpaste commercial white smile just as brilliant as the sun and a dimple on one side. I decided this must be what love looks like, and it certainly must be what love felt like because I could hardly breathe. This had to be it."

Samantha was enjoying every minute as I let her into what she felt was a very secret place. I didn't intend for it to be, but that's how it panned out.

"Did you think it was love right off the bat?" She wanted to know. She was deep-diving, and I was caught in the net. But I didn't mind. Samantha always had a way that was just…well, comfortable. I didn't feel like I was being interrogated.

"Okay, listen carefully, Samantha, because, trust me, I won't be repeating any of this. You know I've been in church all my life. Not in relationship with God, but in church."

Samantha nodded. She was a PK (pastor's kid), and we had many discussions on the whole church thing on different occasions.

"You asked me if it was love right off the bat. I would easily tell you yes, then, because I had no idea what love was. I'm still not sure I know. But he seemed to be everything other people said was right for me. He was handsome, well-spoken, established, very polite, had a sense of humor, and he could spell Jesus, pray, and loved church. JACKPOT!

"Sounds perfect," said Samantha. "That's the stuff dreams are made of."

"I thought so too. That's when I learned about meeting the representative and applying the ninety-day rule. If I had done that, I would never have boarded that train."

Samantha looked at me strangely, so I continued.

"When you first meet people, they are on their best behavior. That courtship thing is serious, and being as naïve as I was, I thought he was a blessing. You know the scripture about how a man who finds a wife finds a good thing? Well, I was the good thing, and I was convinced he had indeed found me."

"What convinced you, Pat?"

"Because that's what he told me. Truth is, he could have told me anything, and I would have believed him. As I recall, we were at dinner one night, and he softly touched my cheek and announced, 'God made you just for me. I knew as soon as I walked into the church that day, you were the wife I had been searching for.' Honey, my ears were burning, and my heart was beating faster than a theme park monorail. Next thing I knew, I was walking down the aisle. And I was happy. But for a veeerrryyy short period of time."

Samantha sighed. "I think about you and the other friends I have. Women I admire. Women I have always viewed as being smart that you can't easily fool."

"Well, that's probably true most of the time. Unfortunately, somehow when it comes to affairs of the heart, we all seem to leave our brains on the nightstand or tuck them away somewhere," I told her.

"I don't mean to be out of line or anything, but you got divorced so quickly. Did you want the marriage to be saved? I mean, how about counseling?" Samantha was relentless.

"I think counseling is a great thing, if both spouses agree. We had counseling before marriage, and I still went down that aisle," I told her. "You know when you get to that place where your mind is set that he's 'The One.' nothing is going to change your mind." I quickly continued. I was ready for this exchange to end. "When I think about it, I'm not sure I was really in love with him as much as I was in love with the idea of him. That's where I got into trouble. I didn't have any idea who I was or what I wanted before I met him. I was lost from the beginning. I just knew I never wanted to be alone, so I thought this was it."

"How do you stay out of that place, though? How do you keep from going down a path that you're unsure of?" Samantha asked under her breath, "Why do you stay on the train when you know you should get off at the next station?"

I decided to treat what I heard as rhetorical and not respond. It was an important conversation for Samantha to have at that moment. It was later that I understood why. Samantha knew me well enough to know I had reached my limit, so she knew not to push. I was certain no answer was the right answer in this case. Whatever I had to offer had the potential to put years of friendship on the wrong track, and I was not willing to risk it. Even still, I had to admit I had enjoyed the day. While the conversation was still warm, the coffee was now growing cold. That was a definite indicator that it was clearly time to get off this train.

CHAPTER 7
Shockwave At The Station

Back at Crown Pavilion, we had been sitting at the table long enough for the shift to change, and we didn't even care. Jean, Charlotte, Diamond, and I sampled every appetizer they had, shared a couple of entrees, and were ready for dessert when Diamond's phone rang.

Charlotte beamed. She was certain it was Diamond's husband checking on her by the way Diamond was smiling. Charlotte longed for the day when someone would check on her that way. Suddenly Diamond gave us a 'shh' motion and removed herself from the table. Her face was not reflective of an 'I Love You' call. She looked really worried as she stepped away.

We all had our own opinion as to what the problem might be.

"I hope there's nothing wrong with one of the kids," said Charlotte.

"She hasn't been out with us long enough to be summoned back home," Jean assessed.

"She just started this work-at-home assignment. Maybe it's that," Charlotte offered.

"Nope," said Jean, "That's not a work-related face. That's a personal problem kind of face."

We all stared in silence as Diamond returned to the table. The look was still intact.

"You all are not going to believe this," said Diamond. "That was Samantha. She's called off the wedding."

We all began to speak at once. What happened? Was something wrong? Was she sick? Was he sick? Was he cheating? Was she cheating? What could break up a seemingly perfect relationship right before the wedding?

Then I remembered my conversation with Samantha several months back and decided this might be a good time to share.

"Maybe this isn't as strange as we think," I said. "I ran into Samantha a little while ago, by accident, really, and we got into a long conversation about relationships and marriage, divorce, all kinds of stuff. I thought she was just going through that premarital thing people go through. I never dreamed it was more than that, but maybe it was."

"So, what do we do?" Charlotte said with tears in her eyes.

"What do *we* do?" Jean asked. "I don't know what you all are going to do, but I'm going to start with a drink. Waiter, we need some help over here."

As the waiter came hurrying over, Jean asked for the wine list, which she instructed him to give to us, while she inquired about some concoction she wanted them to make for her at the bar. We all placed our orders and sat stunned and silent.

Charlotte spoke first. "We can't let this happen. We just can't. Something isn't right.

"Apparently," said Jean. "That's why there isn't going to be a wedding."

"That's not what I mean," said Charlotte. "I just spoke to her the other day. Last week as a matter of fact and she was fine. She couldn't have been happier. Diamond, did she give any reason?"

"No. She told me not to ask her any questions, and I didn't. Funny thing is she was perfectly calm."

"Probably the calm before the storm," Jean commented.

"Where is she?" I asked Diamond.

Diamond only seemed to have enough information to keep the rest of us on edge. Not a good thing. I kept thinking about my last meeting with Samantha. We parted on a high note, but apparently, there was something underlying that never came to the surface. But I didn't need to make anything up. I needed to get to Samantha.

"Diamond, the wedding is supposed to be in two days. How is she planning to break the news to everyone? Is she waiting until Sunday, or is she calling people now?" I asked. I was getting very edgy. "Think, Diamond, think! She must have said something."

As Diamond was shaking her head to indicate that she didn't know anything, Jean had the answer.

"Diamond, look at your phone," Jean said. "Her number will be in the phone. Pat, would she recognize your number?"

"No, she wouldn't. I got a new phone since she and I were together last."

"Great. You call the number Diamond has in her phone and see if she answers."

Every now and then, Jean had the right answer.

Almost as soon as the phone rang, Samantha picked up.

"Hey Samantha, it's me, Pat…No, no, no, don't hang up. I just want to talk to you. I'm glad you're okay, but where are you? Is anybody with you? Okay, I'm glad you're not by yourself…Have you told them yet…Oh, I see. Well, we're on our way…. Me, Diamond, Charlotte, and Jean. We were coming anyway, now we're coming early. If you want whatever is going on to be handled by us rather than you, I suggest you be there when we get there. I'll call you back in about an hour and you better answer the phone. Do you hear me, Samantha? Remember what we said the last time we saw each other. That's right and it still holds so I'll see you soon."

As I hung up the phone, I looked at the trio staring at me and announced, "Okay ladies, change of plans."

CHAPTER 8
New Direction

Team Samantha was ready to board the train for Pikesville and do whatever needed to be done to rescue their Sista. Problem was none of us were sure if she needed rescuing, and if she did, rescuing from what? We were in agreement of one thing: we needed to see her and make sure that she was all right. It was Friday. Her wedding was scheduled for Sunday. Over the phone, she agreed not to do anything until we got to her, and that would either be late tonight or first thing Saturday morning. Remember the train I told you about earlier? That nice *Passenger Train* that took you to that place called THERE? Sunday was the day it would stop at the station, the destination Samantha had wanted to reach. The station she had carefully packed for and planned for. The fact that she was willing to sit tight until we got there was a good sign that she was indecisive. Yes, that was a good sign. Had she been sure, she would not have encouraged us to come and would have been busy telling everyone to stay home because there was not going to be anything happening THERE. What we needed to do was decide how we would get to her and what our strategy would be once we arrived.

While Jean looked up the train schedules, Charlotte was trying to reach her 'boo thang', and Diamond was explaining to her husband why he was going to have to cancel his card game and watch the kids while she set out on an emergency mission to 'Save A Sista' from we knew not what. We were always good in a crisis, and this was a crisis if I ever saw one.

"Okay, the next train for Pikesville leaves at 9:30 pm. That's about three hours from now," Jean said. "It's almost 6:00 pm. Is there any way you all can pull it together and get back here by 9:00 pm?"

Everyone looked at her in amazement. Jean, queen of tardy, had the nerve to suggest the rest of us wouldn't be on time.

"Settle down, y'all, you're wasting time looking at me. I got in yesterday, and I have a suite across the circle from here at Pavilion Towers. I never really unpacked, so I'm good. What about you, Charlotte?"

"I'm still trying to get my honey on the phone, but I can't reach him."

"I'm not surprised," Jean said under her breath. I kicked her under the table. Charlotte didn't notice and continued, "But you know what? I'll just keep calling to let him know what's happening. I hope he won't be too upset."

"He'll be alright, I promise," Jean said. "Diamond, are you in?"

"It's going to be tight for me, but I think I can do it. If it looks like I can't make the 9:30 pm train tonight, I'll take the train we planned to catch at 6:30 am tomorrow. I'll just keep in touch by phone. Come on, Charlotte. I'll drop you off, and we'll work it out." We quickly gathered our things and hurried out of the Crown Pavilion, chattering away.

"Well, it looks like we are right back where we started," I told Jean. "What time should I meet you at the station?"

"How about 8:30 pm?" said Jean.

I called the waiter over to see what I could do about the check. Charlotte and Diamond must have forgotten their beverage tab, but no worries.

"You go ahead. I've got the check, and I'll text you the gate number," Jean said in her matter-of-fact manner as she shooed me away from the table.

"I won't argue," I told her. "I can get an Uber to my house. My bag is already packed for tomorrow, so I can scoop it up and take the same Uber and meet you back here."

"Perfect! See you in a couple of hours."

I headed for the door and glanced over at the bar. Lo and behold, there he was, Charlotte's love. He was sitting with a gorgeous woman who was way too close to be a friend, colleague, or associate. Good grief, I thought, not again. Charlotte had shown us his picture, and there he was, in the flesh.

I was too preoccupied with everything else to give this much thought though. As soon as I got outside, my Uber driver was already turning the corner. And I was reeling, thinking of Samantha not getting married. But it wasn't just me; all of us were. She always had a way of bringing us together. A lot of times, she was the safety net for everybody: her family, folks she worked with, church family…I mean everybody. But as happy and solid as she appeared to be, there was an empty place inside

Samantha that she was almost afraid to fill. I think the day we ran into each other and talked was the closest she had come to exposing whatever pain was in her past. One of the last things she said to me that day was, "You gotta protect yourself. No one wants to be hurt." As I continued rolling that conversation over in my head, I kept trying to remember any clues she might have been leaving. But clues to what? None of us knew what was going on. I started getting a little anxious. I wanted Samantha to be happy—all of us did. But more importantly, I wanted her to be whole. That day, she seemed to be in search of something to fill a void, but I don't think she ever really got what she was searching for, and now…well, now I just knew I had to get to my friend.

The ride didn't take me long, and on the way, I decided to call Charlotte and see what was going on with her and Diamond first. Forty-five minutes had passed already, so I thought I'd better check in. Charlotte picked up on the first ring.

"Hey lady," I said.

"Oh, it's just you," Charlotte quickly answered.

"Thanks a lot." I could tell by the sound of her voice there was trouble in paradise.

"I haven't heard from my boo," Charlotte said. She had an exasperated sound in her voice, mingled in with a tinge of anxiety. "Do you think he's alright?"

You better believe he's alright, I thought. Better than alright, as a matter of fact. I just saw him chatting up a beautiful, chocolate head-turner with long dark hair and blonde highlights, and he looked fine to me. That's what I was thinking, but I didn't dare say it. I was a chicken friend right now with a more important agenda.

"I'm sure all is well. Have you made it home yet? "Are you and Diamond still on schedule?" I asked. Something told me one of them, if not both, would be arriving in the morning, which was perfectly fine with me. Samantha's drama was the only one I wanted to be concerned about between now and Sunday. Charlotte would have to wait. "Have you talked to Diamond since she dropped you off? Is she going to pick you up on the way back?"

"Hold on, Pat, I've got a call coming in. Maybe that's him," said an excited Charlotte.

I immediately hung up. I just couldn't entertain it. I decided to call Jean and see if she had heard from Diamond.

Jean answered the phone on the second ring.

"Hey Jean. Have you heard anything from Diamond?"

"Pat, your timing is scary. I just hung up the phone. She's coming in the morning like she planned. One of the kids is sick, and she doesn't feel right about leaving him with hubby. Her mom was already scheduled to watch them tomorrow, so she's fine with that."

"Well, that will cancel Charlotte for tonight. She won't leave without Diamond, and right now, she's still on the hunt for her one and only."

"God has a way of working things out," Jean said, breathing a sigh of relief. "How far are you?"

"About five minutes from my house, and like I said, it will be a quick turnaround. I should be back no later than 8:30 pm."

"Okay, come to Track 16 when you get here. I'll be waiting." There was a long pause; then Jean said, "Hey Pat, whatever it is, Samantha's going to be okay, right?"

"Sure, she is," I reassured Jean, then added, "Sure, she is," for myself.

These were the times you called upon the Lord. I knew God knows everything; I mean, I truly believed that. What was the likelihood we would all be together when the call came? Why did I see Charlotte's fiancé when I was leaving? This was Friday evening. There was no traffic, going or coming. It was if God had time stand still to accommodate us as we set about on this adventure. I felt it might be emotionally taxing for all of us to descend on Samantha tonight, but He took care of that too. I just didn't understand why all this was happening. I wanted to ask God why—you know how easily you can get into asking God why; certainly, all of this was just crazy—but He was not talking. I prayed all the way back to the train station. I was really concerned, but I just felt God was with her. He was the Conductor on her train right now, and He knew just what to do. The real question was what we were supposed to do when we got there.

I don't know how many text messages were sent between the four of us in that short amount of time but everything we needed to do; we did. And so, Jean and I left on the 9:15 pm train. Samantha had told us she would be waiting for us when we spoke to her earlier. She seemed reasonably calm under the circumstances so that made each of us feel better. We got some coffee while we waited, snacked on a soft pretzel, and waited patiently for those two familiar words.

"All Aboard."

Those two words had the same effect on me that they always did. I had butterflies, but this time it was because I wasn't sure what the future would hold at the end of the ride. Right now, I was just happy Jean got us seats together. I wanted to pick her brain about what I saw leaving the lunch venue to go home and get my bag. There seemed to be a lot going on, a lot of questions for which no one had answers, at least none that made sense. While I should have been exhausted, I was wired and wide awake. Adrenalin, caffeine, or God knows what was kicking in. Sleep was nowhere in my future. Before I could start a conversation with Jean, my phone rang. It was Samantha.

"Hey lady, how are you holding up?" I asked.

"As well as can be expected, I guess. Have you all boarded the train yet?" Samantha asked.

"Actually, it's just me and Jean."

"What happened to Diamond and Charlotte?' Samantha asked. "I thought you all were coming together."

"Why they aren't coming tonight is a longer story than I have time to tell, and I'd be making most of it up anyway."

Samantha chuckled. That was a good sign.

"To be painfully honest, I'm glad it's just going to be you and Jean. I'm not sure I want to sort through what's packed in my baggage with Charlotte being on the verge of getting married." Samantha seemed quite clear, considering what she was about to do. I thought she would be hysterical because this was a train wreck if I ever saw one. If she was on the verge of losing it, it wasn't coming through. "I wanted to let you know I'm having a car pick you up at the station and bring you to the hotel."

"Samantha, we can handle that," I said.

"I know you can but let me do this. I pray the train will be on time, but I'll keep checking so you won't be waiting when you get here. Do you think you all will want something to eat, or perhaps some snacks or something?"

I realized Samantha needed something to do to keep herself in a good headspace, so preparing for our arrival and checking train schedules had the winning tickets in the 'stay calm' lottery. I let her do what she needed to do and told her we would see her soon.

When Jean and I got settled, I wasted no time in getting down to business.

"Jean, remember when we were at lunch and Charlotte shared a picture of her new love?"

Jean nodded in the affirmative.

"I swear Charlotte's fiancé looks like someone I've seen before."

"That's because you have," said Jean carefully. "Do you remember going to Dot's last Fall?"

"Sure," I responded. "It was the best party of the season."

"Do you remember the discussion over why she had invited her ex to the party?" Jean didn't say another word. She just sat there waiting for me to catch up. When I finally did, I did all I could do to keep from screaming.

"Oh my God, oh my God, oh my God. That's Dot's ex? Do you think Charlotte knows?"

"Do you think Charlotte cares?" asked Jean.

"Jean, which door did you go out of when you left the train station?"

"The one closest to the exit by the hotel, why?"

That was no help at all.

"Was that the one near the bar area?" I asked.

"If you're asking if I saw old what's his name with that gorgeous woman, yes, I did," she said.

I know my eyes were big as saucers as I asked Jean, "What are we going to do about it?"

"About what?" Jean wanted to know.

"About Charlotte?" I asked.

Jean was adamant when she responded: "What about Charlotte? Pat, we are not going there. At least, I'm not. That is Charlotte and her little red wagon. It has nothing to do with us. You saw how she responded when I even tried to question her about him. No, thanks, ma'am. You're on your own with this one."

I knew Jean was right. But I didn't want to see Charlotte hurt.

"Okay, Jean, let me ask you this. If you were in Charlotte's shoes, wouldn't you want to know?"

"I can't even imagine because I would never be in Charlotte's place."

"But if you were, wouldn't you want to know?" I insisted.

"Knowing and believing and doing something about it are all very different things, Pat."

"I know, but somehow I think we're damned if we do and damned if we don't."

"Exactly, so I'd much rather pretend I have no knowledge. Besides, Pat, how many people do you need to rescue in one weekend?"

"I'm not trying to rescue anyone; I just hate watching train wrecks—"

"Okay, now I have a question for you," interjected Jean.

I knew I would get a turn in the hot seat, so I was already preparing my answer.

"Would you want to know? If you were in Charlotte's shoes, would you want to know?" she asked. My answer wasn't cut and dry, and Jean knew that, but she wasn't going to change the parameters of her question and what she expected as a response. "Pat, it's a simple question with a simple answer—yes or no. Either, yes, you would; or no, you would not."

Jean thought she had me trapped, so she took a sip of her coffee and settled back in her seat.

"My answer is yes and no," I replied. "Yes, I would want to know, and no, I would not want my friend to be the one to tell me. I wouldn't want to be able to deny the findings. I wouldn't want to be in a position where he could excuse it away or even tell me my friend was mistaken. I would want to get the information in an undeniable, irrefutable way."

Jean sighed and said, "I should have known better than to ask anyone vaguely associated with the law."

"But again," I said with confidence, "I'm not Charlotte."

I almost had Jean convinced that Charlotte should know, but who should tell her was an entirely different story. She didn't think it should be either one of us.

"Pat, I don't think we should get into it and especially not this weekend. I also don't want to argue about it. I feel we have enough going on with Samantha."

In the end, I got Jean to agree not to delve into it this weekend. I considered that a victory. When I decided to close my eyes for a moment, I soon heard a sound that seemed to be very far away, saying, "Pat, wake up." It was just close enough to let me know my power nap had indeed come to an end.

"Gather up your things, kiddo. We have arrived," said Jean as she gathered up hers. I opened my eyes and saw she was checking her make-up. It was close to midnight. Who does that?

Just like Samantha said there would be, we were greeted with a gentleman holding a sign that indicated he was our driver. We exchanged pleasantries and started towards the hotel. We were careful in our conversation, not really knowing if he was a true driver or a friend. We definitely didn't want to cause Samantha any embarrassment.

The driver, whose name was Ted, let us know that Samantha wanted us to call her as soon as he picked us up. We were obedient to do exactly that. Then she asked if she could stop by our room if we weren't too tired. Too tired? Are you kidding me? We had just taken a train and an almost thirty-minute car ride to get to her, and she thought we were going to be too tired to talk to her tonight? Oh yes, there was something wrong for sure.

CHAPTER 9
Arrival

We got to the hotel, and of course, it was beautiful. Jean and I wondered how Samantha had found such a beautiful venue in such a hick town. What I didn't realize was this was about to turn into the longest night of my life.

We got off the elevator only to see Samantha coming down the hall in a fluffy, white robe and spa slippers. We hurried to greet her and were met with hugs and tears. There was no conversation at all, nothing but an assurance that we were together, and that meant victory.

It was a little awkward because we had no idea what we had actually come to do other than support our friend. Samantha had almost become a professional passenger. She was always riding the *Relationship Train* but never getting anywhere. This time, though, seemed to be different. She knew this train was headed for the altar, and she was ready. What changed? What happened within the last year that made her not want to marry this incredible man? Her soulmate? She had to spill the beans and do it tonight.

As we entered the room, we asked Samantha how she was doing and if there was anything we could do to help.

"My biggest concern is letting everyone know ahead of time," said Samantha. "Oh, and I had a surprise for you all. This was going to be a wedding/reunion. Pat already knows part of it. I had gotten in touch with Dot, Jackie, and Teresa and tried to get them to come. Teresa said she would make every effort to attend. Dot was going to be out of the country. I haven't heard back from Jackie, but I'll try one more time. I didn't want them to travel to a wedding that was not going to happen." She gave a deep sigh, and we just sat quietly.

We settled in and gave what we felt was the appropriate amount of time before addressing the elephant in the room. And the horror story of Samantha's ride began. No one would have guessed that she had been ill. That her fiancé was a functioning alcoholic. That there was physical and emotional abuse. That our Samantha, our strong, competent, beautiful Samantha, had already attempted to take her life. That she lived with fear and endured pain. No one would have guessed, but tonight no one had to. Tonight, Samantha told it all.

As she began the story of her time with Joshua, it became apparent that it was a story of a love gone wrong from the beginning.

"Where did you meet him anyway?" Jean asked. "I can't really remember. He just was sort of always around."

"You're right," said Samantha. "Even before we started dating officially, he was at the church helping my father, or helping to move something, or taking something or somebody somewhere. He was always there, and we were grateful. One little flirtation grew into another, then another, and next thing I knew, we were talking about marriage."

I reminded Samantha and Jean about an earlier conversation we had about how sometimes that train to THERE can move along quicker than you want it to. We laughed about how Samantha managed to end the relationship with Joshua…that time.

"Honey, I remember when you called and told us you got off that train at the station in that imaginary place called 'good sense' and didn't look back. We all breathed a sigh of relief on that one. But you know, Samantha, you never said why you broke up or why you went back," I said.

Samantha replied, "Well, the breakup part wasn't tough for me. If you cheat before you get married, there is no reason to think you won't cheat after. Third time around, I'd had enough."

"All of that sounds good, but why did you take him back?"

"You know how it goes, Pat. He came back with a sob story, and I believed him. When I look back on it, though, I never really actually did. I just wanted to. Every time we broke up, I would meet someone new. Each encounter was worse than the last. Joshua must have had some kind of homing device, because whenever I was at the point of saying to my new man, 'Joker, you've got to go, I am not settling, you are not The One,' Joshua would text or come by, or call, or send flowers and I'd fall back into the trap which usually had a different trick attached."

"Truth is," I told her, "You didn't stop settling at all. You just traded one dysfunctional wannabe for another.

But the last time you and I talked, I thought things were fine, and everything was going well."

"I thought so too," said Samantha as her eyes welled up with tears.

Jean could be counted on to get right to the point. "Okay, Samantha, so what happened this time?"

"It started when we began really planning for the wedding—there was one disagreement after another. Then the arguments escalated. The yelling became a push, which became a shove, which became a slap, and I think you know the rest of the story. All very predictable."

"Oh, Samantha, you never said—"

"I know, Pat. I didn't know how. I'd been dealing with it, but I knew I couldn't do this as part of my forever after. I just couldn't do it. Surprisingly Joshua took it quite well. In fact, he totally agreed with me. He understood, and we agreed this was best for everyone, so there you have it."

Jean and I looked at each other, not knowing how to respond, but Samantha did it for us.

"Ladies, it's all good," she said as she looked at her watch and back at us with her soft Samantha smile. It was almost 4:00 am, and all of us were exhausted. "Here's what we're going to do. We're going to get some sleep. Joshua is going to be here in about an hour to pick up a few things he left behind."

Jean shook her head. "Samantha, I don't think that's a good idea. A lot of emotional stuff has gone down in the last twenty-four hours, and I don't feel the same as I used to about your fiancé. Why can't he get whatever it is later in the day when more people are around?"

"That's exactly why," said Samantha. "He doesn't want to face anyone. I wanted to leave him with a little dignity."

"Samantha, I'm with Jean on this one. Meeting him is not a good idea.

"It's fine," said Samantha, "Trust me, okay?"

Samantha stood up, yawned, stretched, and opened her arms wide. We both fell into one of the best hugs ever and then waved as she headed down the hall to take the elevator to her room.

We quietly closed the door. There was nothing else to say. We both fell across our respective beds without a word.

I don't know when I fell asleep. I only remember waking up to screaming in the distance, to the sound of two loud pops, then silence, then to two more pops, then screams again. But these screams were my voice in concert with Jean's as we yelled in unison, "SAMAN-THA!"

CHAPTER 10
The End Of The Line

At first, we were immobilized. Then we moved in what seemed like slow motion to get to the door and open it, trying to see and hear what was going on. Even though the sun wasn't quite up on the horizon, people were up and opening the doors to their rooms like zombies in a badly written version of The Walking Dead. While they were still deciding whether to come out or go back in, Jean and I opted to throw on some clothes and find Samantha. Before I could really say anything, Jean was on her cell phone, frantically dialing Samantha, and began shaking her head. No answer. Jean had that I-knew-something-wasn't-right look on her face. It's the one she uses just before she says, "I told you so!" But there was no time for that.

When we went to the door again, half-dressed and looking like two lunatics, it was pandemonium. People were everywhere, running, screaming, trying to ask anyone they could what was going on. We noticed security scrambling and talking on their headsets, but we couldn't make out what they were saying. Then the deafening sounds of police sirens and ambulances were right below us. The first set of responders got on the elevator. Jean managed to get close enough to security to overhear, "They're on their way up…four shots…a couple on the twenty-first floor…one critical…I don't think the other one is going to make it."

Security disappeared into the next already crowded elevator while we stood speechless, stunned, wondering what to do next. Samantha was staying on the twenty-first floor, and we had to get there. We were on the fifteenth floor and waiting for an elevator was going to take way too long. Without a word, we looked at each other, saw the exit sign for the stairs simultaneously, and headed towards it. By the time we reached the seventeenth floor, we were both so winded we thought perhaps it would be the perfect time to borrow one or two of those paramedics and an oxygen tank for ourselves. Instead, we decided to sit on the stairs, gather our thoughts and catch our breath.

Jean looked at me and said as she gasped for air, "What were we thinking?" She tried not to act as if she could hardly breathe. "We are not as young as we used to be, but we've got to find out what's happening." And with that, adrenaline kicked in like a tidal wave that swept us up the remaining flights of stairs.

The corridor was chaotic, and we did everything we could to inch our way through, but to no avail. So, we did the next best thing and began to scream, "That's our friend!"

No one seemed to care, though. In fact, they tightened up even more to keep us from passing, so we screamed even louder as tears of frustration began to flow.

"Samantha! SAMANTHA!"

We were almost at the point of collapsing when the police began telling us to move back, as they brought a stretcher out with the body bag. I couldn't tell you if the minutes seemed like hours, or if it took hours that seemed like minutes, I just know that Jean and I embraced each other and fell apart, whispering her name.

Then we heard another whisper, "Hey guys, what's going on?"

Through the tears, chaos, and confusion, there stood Samantha, sipping a cup of coffee.

Jean and I looked back and forth at each other, then back and forth at Samantha. We grabbed her and screamed, but with joy this time! We were talking over each other so quickly.

"Where were you—?"

"We've been looking everywhere—"

"Where's Joshua—?"

"What happened—?"

"We heard gunshots—"

"Why didn't you answer the phone—?"

"Isn't that your room—?"

As much commotion as we were creating, no one was paying any attention to us at all. I was so glad because we must have looked ridiculous in that hallway. Between frustration, tears, questions, nothing was better than embracing Samantha and knowing she was okay. Samantha, on the other hand, was totally bewildered, and I think somewhat amused at us and the adventure we had been on trying to make sure she was safe.

As responders and security began to clear the hallway and cut through the confusion, Samantha gave the first utterance of sanity.

"Jean and Pat, stop. Just stop! Let's go back to your room. There is a freight elevator around the corner. We can get on it, go downstairs, make it to your room, and you can fully explain why you're in this corridor looking like you look."

We looked at each other, agreed, and made it to the elevator as quickly as we could. When we got to the room, the message light was flashing on the phone. Jean decided to check the messages while I talked to Samantha. We knew it had to be Diamond and Charlotte, and we were right. They had been calling non-stop. Just as they were boarding the train, there was a breaking news story about a shooting at the hotel where we were staying. They assumed the same thing Jean and I had, that Samantha was somehow involved, and it was not good news. Jean reassured Charlotte, everything was fine, and it was okay for Diamond to stop praying. Jean let them know everything would be explained when they arrived.

"I can't tell you how worried we were about you," I told Samantha. "When we heard gunshots, we both thought that, well, maybe things hadn't gone well between you and Joshua when he came to pick up his things."

"Oh, my Lord," Samantha said with dismay. "You can't be serious. I told you everything was fine."

"Well, how can you blame us?" I said defensively. "So much stuff goes on when people break up, and your account of Joshua wasn't exactly glowing."

Samantha hesitated, then agreed, "You're right, and I didn't really fill in all the blanks."

"There were blanks?" Jean questioned as she hung up the phone. "It all seemed pretty clear to me. He became abusive. It was time to go!"

"It wasn't quite that easy. It never is," explained Samantha. "I had fallen into the trap a lot of women do. You know, he loves me, he didn't mean it, somehow it was my fault..."

"And you were falling for it hook line and sinker," Jean added with a hint of disdain.

I was about to add my two cents when Samantha raised her hand in a gesture that let me know she could handle whatever was coming. She walked over to the window and pulled the drapes to let in the sun. She tilted her head up and closed her eyes for a moment as if to take in the warmth of the sunlight. Then she crossed her arms and took her moment.

I laid across the bed, Jean sat cross-legged in the overstuffed chair, and we waited. It took a few minutes, but when Samantha turned around, she was ready to tell it all, and we were ready to listen to whatever she had to say.

"I wasn't totally honest about my decision to not let this be a part of my forever life," Samantha said. "In fact, I was the one trying to hold on. I didn't want to admit I was wrong again. I didn't want to have to say, 'I almost made it,' again. Everything was moving along faster and faster, and I didn't have the courage to slow things down, let alone stop the momentum. I didn't want to get off that train we're always talking about. It was Joshua who put on the brakes. We had a long talk one night a few weeks back. We were brutally honest with one another about some untruths during our pre-marital counseling. Joshua hadn't dealt with some things in his past that were triggering his outbursts, and he knew it. It wasn't all him. I had unresolved issues of my own that needed to be dealt with. One night we committed to finding the right therapists or counselors so we could get the help we needed. Not as a couple, but as individuals, and that's where we are now. But one thing we could not do was enter into a covenant relationship we had no business being in."

"Covenant relationship? I've never heard you mention that..." I was looking at Samantha as I spoke. I mean, REALLY looking at her. She was in this strangely peaceful place that I couldn't quite figure out and clearly had not counted on. When I looked at Jean, I knew she noticed it too. Before Jean could speak, Samantha, as if a psychic sense kicked in, continued what seemed like a well-constructed podcast.

"Okay, now I need you to get a grip for this next part," Samantha said with a smile. "During the premarital counseling I talked about, something changed for both of us. We rededicated our lives to Christ. I know it sounds corny, but we did. The closer we drew to Him, the more we realized a wedding for us right now would just not be the right thing to do. Now, you know it all, and you two are probably the only ones who truly have the full story."

Then there was only silence.

I had nothing to say, and Jean had nothing to offer except, "As fancy as this hotel is, you'd think there would be Kleenex readily available." Then she uncrossed her legs and went searching.

We had all been fighting back tears for our own reasons; now it was time to let them flow freely, and we did. Every tear seemed to help wash away some pain of the past. We dealt with our individual feelings and fears that morning. We talked about our hopes, dreams, and disappointments; love found and love lost; abuse and addictions; neglect, bad choices, being sidetracked, getting back on track with victory, courage, and all things good. Each of us knew a part, but no one knew the whole. We discovered we had been passengers on any number of trains but still had not arrived THERE. We also realized that in all the time we had known each other, we very seldom, if ever, talked about our faith or the things of God unless there was a crisis. And you know what baffles me the most? Without coercion or conversation, as if we had taken a blood oath and sworn each other to secrecy, there were some things about that night, private things we shared that we never spoke of again, not ever.

While Jean, Samantha, and I were having our transparent moments and baring our souls at the hotel, Diamond and Charlotte were having moments of their own on the train. Diamond had always been one to take it to the Lord and leave it there. She also had a way of getting you to see things differently. She had the most influence on Charlotte, and that was evident when they arrived. During the back-and-forth conversations that Jean was monitoring, we agreed Diamond and Charlotte would call when they arrived, and we would meet in the hotel restaurant. It seemed like food solved all issues for us, and we didn't mind one bit.

Samantha returned to her room after cleaning out a tissue box and sharing a few more hugs while Jean and I decided on a power nap. As soon as my head hit the pillow, the phone rang. I answered to the sound of Charlotte saying, "We're here!"—in her outside voice, I might add. She told me where they were and that we needed to, "Hurry down!" Jean yawned, stretched, and turned the clock around to check the time. That's when I noticed my power nap had been almost two hours long!

It took us forever to get downstairs. Jean didn't care; she was going to be flawless if it took her until midnight. Fortunately, it didn't, but when she stepped off the elevator, she owned the space. Samantha, Charlotte, and Diamond were on the other side of the room, engaged in a rather serious conversation. We found out later Samantha met them earlier and calmed all their fears about the wedding cancellation, all in her own way. I'm not sure what she said, but all seemed to be well because when Charlotte spotted us, she came running towards us, as best she could in her five-inch heels and teeny tiny dress. I gave Jean a knowing look and thought to myself, "Poor Charlotte. What's she going to do when she finds out about her new fiancé?" Well, poor Charlotte had news for us. As we were laughing about something that happened the last time we were all together, Jean was the first to get everyone's attention.

"Ladies, grab your glasses and let's have a toast," she said with a broad smile.

We all grabbed our glasses, and Charlotte said in her clueless voice, "This is so much fun, but what are we toasting?"

Realizing she had nothing planned, Jean said, "I don't know. Let's toast to Saturday."

"Saturday, it is then," said Charlotte raising her glass.

Jean noticed before anyone else did. She grabbed Charlotte's left hand and, in wide-eyed amazement, said, "That must have been some train ride. Where's the ring?"

My jaw dropped. Charlotte looked back and forth to see who was watching this drama unfold. "Jean, calm down, and Pat, you have got to close your mouth, honey. My ring is upstairs, but I won't be putting it back on. I won't be getting married, at least not now, and definitely not to him. I value myself way more than that." She and Diamond clinked glasses in their own private toast. Samantha continued to look in the other direction, I finally closed my mouth, and Jean was, believe it or not, speechless!

Two 'no wedding' announcements in one weekend were way too much for me to handle. I could only say two words, but I said them loud enough to have been heard at the train station: "WHAT HAPPENED?"

Everything and everybody in the room stopped and looked our way. I started coughing and waving my hands, saying, "I'm okay," in a feeble attempt to cover my outburst. When things returned to normal in the room, I pleaded, "Will somebody please tell us what's going on?"

Diamond and Charlotte looked at each other and began talking at the same time as Samantha continued to look in the opposite direction.

"Will one of you talk?" Jean said through clenched teeth. "Just ONE." She could hardly stand the suspense, and I was right there with her.

"I'm not sure I want to know, though," I said.

"Well, I want to know, and it looks like Ms. Samantha over there already knows." Samantha tilted her head and gave a knowing wink which put us all at ease.

"So, who's going first?"

Diamond spoke up. "Well, Charlotte. It's your story, and I think you should be the one to tell it."

"I don't mind if I do," said Charlotte with pride, and tell it she did.

I won't recount all of it here, but the short version is Charlotte discovered her value on that train. It seems she passed the same scenario Jean and I saw leaving the Imperial station: her fiancé with another woman. Their affection was obvious, and Charlotte was devastated. She decided to talk to Diamond and be transparent. The astonishing thing was Diamond was able to do in a train ride what we had wanted to do for years: help Charlotte believe in who she was, the beautiful woman God created her to be—the one who deserved the best; the one who deserved love; the one who would be patient and not settle for anything or anybody from that day forward.

Charlotte ended her recounting by standing and making a four-word announcement: "Ladies, I am free!" We all applauded sincerely and without reservation. At that point, Jean moved around the table to where Charlotte was standing, wrapped Charlotte in her arms, and said, "I am some kind of proud of you today."

Charlotte suddenly, but gently, stepped back from Jean and, holding her by the shoulders, said, "Why, Jean, are your eyes leaking? I believe they are."

We all waited, that pregnant pause people talk about, and Jean shrugged her shoulders in exasperation and said, "Can't anybody find a box of tissue in this place?"

We erupted into laughter, yet again.

It had turned out to be a beautiful day, with a wonderful sense of joy and peace filling the atmosphere. That wasn't unusual when we all got together but there was something about this time that was different. Despite what could have been tragic, it looked like we had all taken the Disney railroad to Fantasy Land, and we were happy, happy, happy.

But how could that be? We were supposed to be here on a 'Save My Sista' campaign and uplift Samantha from the pain we thought she must be carrying. Instead, we all sort of saved each other as we celebrated being phenomenal women who could let go of some baggage, travel light, not be railroaded into anything, and arrive right where we were supposed to be…a little bruised perhaps, but none the worse for wear.

They say that people are in your life for a reason, a season, or a lifetime. Our lives covered all the bases. At times, we were seasonal and would lose touch. Other times, we would reach out to each other for support during the good, the bad, and the ugly. But I guess you could say we were lifetime friends who knew how to handle the reasons and seasons we encountered.

I look back over that weekend with contentment. I shared with my friends my thoughts on life and trains. They were happy to discuss the trains we had boarded on our respective journeys, the roads we had traveled, and the passengers we had become.

While we talked, and laughed, and cried our way through those few days, none of us could deny that as unique, strong, and wise as we perceived ourselves to be, or perhaps I should say we were becoming, we were not alone. There were Jeffrey's, Fred's, and Joshua's who were always traveling with us, wanting what we wanted, and not always making the right connection at the right time, whether they admitted it or not.

This quiet time was an exercise in self-discovery to reflect on our travels through life that yielded something else. We began to see the hand of God at work in our lives. We did not orchestrate that weekend. Samantha's cancellation, Charlotte's revelation, Diamond's prayers, Jean's elation, and my train station—only a supreme all-knowing God could have put it all together. Those who were supposed to be in that hotel were there. Those who were not, did not show. He knew who would, and He knew who wouldn't, and He knew what we needed. God has been on every train we have ever traveled, and He has the trip tickets for our lives. With all the names of trains we boarded and the destinations we tried to reach, all we ever wanted was to love, be loved in return, and make others happy in the process.

The joy and fulfillment you look for on previous paths to THERE are found in great measure when you are on the train marked BLESSED. You don't have to wait to get THERE. Every day is complete in and of itself. Every day brings you the peace and joy of intangibles that never run out. Every day you will have exactly what you need because when it's all said and done, THERE is where God is.

ACKNOWLEDGEMENTS

Acknowledging those who journey with you is one of the most difficult tasks to accomplish. You always run the risk of forgetting someone who has played a part in getting you from one stop to another on your way to THERE.

I pray that if you fall into that category, you know who you are and all the things you've done. I also pray that you know how much you are loved and appreciated, even though you may not see your name listed here. But in obedience, I acknowledge the following with gratitude:

Spiritual leaders Bishop Ronald L. Godbee and Pastor Karla Godbee, thank you for opening doors and allowing me to laugh my way to the other side. Your prayers are life to me.

Pastors Valarie and Steve Sims, who have come to know me well and love me still, your prayers and support are invaluable.

Oldest and dearest friends, Pastor Gloria Kennedy and Marylen Jennings Temple, who have remained a part of all that makes me who I am; the good, the bad, and the ugly.

To my newest prayer partners and passengers on this train, Ruth E. Griffin and Victoria Henderson Poole, together we have found new places in God. And yes, He is amazing!

To my family nucleus, Lynn, Jazzmen, Christian, Tracie and Tyler, I thank God for allowing me to be Mommy, Nanny and GiGi. These are titles I cherish as much as I cherish each one of you. Always remember love is a gift to be given unconditionally.

For the supportive, honest cheerleaders on my journey, I thank you. For the foes who pushed me by way of their lack of faith in the God who said, "Yes, you can," I thank you as well.

To the travelers on the train and those waiting at the station, let the love and peace of Almighty God govern and guide you to fulfill your purpose and see His promises come to pass.

ABOUT THE AUTHOR

Andrea L. Hines
Mother, Grandmother, Author, Poet, Speaker,
Entrepreneur, Doctor of Divinity, Certified Life Coach,
and Radio Host

This lady of many talents is a native of Washington, D.C., who now resides in Raleigh, NC. She often says that moving to the "quiet beauty of the Carolinas" deepened her relationship with God and caused her creativity to flow freely."

Andrea has over thirty years of experience train the performing arts as an actor, playwright, and director, with work including performances in numerous community theatre and film projects. She has been a narrator for the North Carolina Library for the Blind and Physically

Handicapped; and continues to enjoy lending her voice to any number of voice-over projects.

Her poetic work has been featured in local newspapers, on Blue Mountain Arts greeting cards and products, and included in numerous anthologies. She has written a collection of inspirational verses titled 'When He Whispers', and words of encouragement inspired by her granddaughter titled, 'Nanny Nuggets'. Her book When Life Speaks brings Inspiration through Affirmations. While Andrea has authored story poems, greeting cards and other works, she says God has given her the ability to write the words people often think but can't express.

She introduced her company, A's Accents in 1994. Her performance and product showcase, "...A Work in Progress.," weaves a story of life experiences through her original verses with musical interludes. "A Reading for His Glory" provides a more intimate atmosphere with smaller groups, giving them the opportunity to interact with the author on a more personal level. Her style and ability to uplift the heart has made her a favorite speaker in areas from commencement exercises to conferences. She is owner of ALH Broadcasting Internet Radio/TV, an affiliate of the Streaming Inspirational Broadcast Network. She cohosts Authors Up with Ruth Griffin and Victoria Henderson-Poole; hosts When Life Speaks; and offers verses of victory on her program "8@8". The When Life Speaks Newsletter is another offering available to subscribers the first Monday of every month. In addition, Andrea is frequently "the voice of the poet" on CYM radio.

Andrea has received an honorary Doctorate Degree of Divinity and is an Elder at the River Church in Durham, NC. She is a Certified Life Coach and owner of C.L.A.S.S Coaching and Consulting-Cultivating Lives and Success Strategies. She believes God has blessed her with certain gifts and only hopes that whatever she creates will be to His glory and a blessing to someone else.